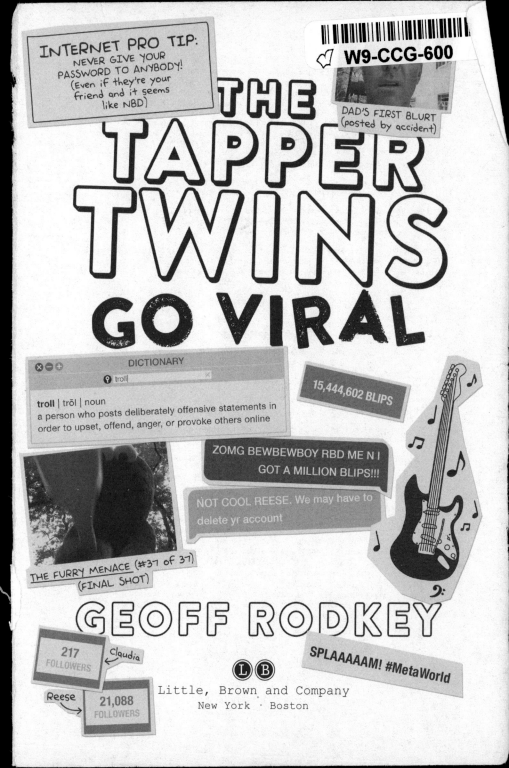

Little, Brown and Company
Hachette Book Group
1290 Avenue of the Americas, New York, NY 10104
Visit us at LBYR.com

Originally published in hardcover and ebook by
Little, Brown and Company in April 2017

First Trade Paperback Edition: March 2018

Little, Brown and Company is a division of Hachette Book Group, Inc.
The Little, Brown name and logo are trademarks of Hachette Book Group, Inc.

The publisher is not responsible for websites (or their content)
that are not owned by the publisher.

Additional copyright/credits information is on page 243.

The Library of Congress has cataloged the hardcover edition as follows:
Names: Rodkey, Geoff, 1970- author.
Title: The Tapper twins go viral / Geoff Rodkey.
Description: First edition. | New York ; Boston : Little, Brown and Company, 2016. | Series: [Tapper twins ; 4] | Summary: "Twelve-year-old twins Reese and Claudia Tapper race to become more popular on social media sites in order to win a high-stakes bet"— Provided by publisher.
Identifiers: LCCN 2015040156| ISBN 9780316297844 (paper over board) | ISBN 9780316268301 (ebook) | ISBN 9780316380393 (library edition ebook)
Subjects: | CYAC: Brothers and sisters—Fiction. | Twins—Fiction. | Social media—Fiction. | Popularity—Fiction. | Family life—New York (State)—New York— Fiction. | New York (N.Y.)—Fiction. | Humorous stories.
Classification: LCC PZ7.R61585 Tav 2016 | DDC [Fic]—dc23
LC record available at http://lccn.loc.gov/2015040156

ISBNs: 978-0-316-47893-9 (pbk.), 978-0-316-26830-1 (ebook)

Printed in the United States of America

LSC-C

10 9 8 7 6 5 4 3 2

THE OFFICIAL HISTORY OF A BUNCH OF
COMPLETELY INSANE THINGS THAT HAPPENED
TO MY BROTHER AND ME ON THE INTERNET
including
SOME VERY HELPFUL TIPS ABOUT HOW TO ACT ONLINE
(+ HOW <u>NOT</u> TO ACT!!!)

compiled as a public service
to other 12-year-olds by
CLAUDIA TAPPER

from interviews with:
Reese Tapper
Sophie Koh
Xander Billington
Carmen Gutierrez
Parvati Gupta
James Mantolini
Jens Kuypers
Akash Gupta
Athena Cohen
Wyatt Templeman
Kalisha Hendricks
Toby Zimmerman
Dimitri Sharansky

And anyone else I forgot

For further information, contact:
Claudia Tapper
Instagram: @claudaroo

CONTENTS

PROLOGUE

**CLAUDIA TAPPER, author of this book/
6th grade class president/
future singer-songwriter**

If you think about it, the Internet
is pretty amazing. It's basically one giant
network with all of human existence on it.
Plus a bunch of cat pictures.

OMG ADORABLE!
(I googled "cute cat pic"—got 23,000,000 results)

But the Internet isn't ALL good. Because human existence isn't all good.

In fact, some of human existence is dark and horrible and disturbing.

This is why you have to be VERY CAREFUL about what you do online. For example, if you click on the wrong link and download a virus...you could destroy your whole computer. (This ACTUALLY HAPPENED to my grandmother.)

INTERNET PRO TIP:
If you aren't 100% sure where a link/file came from,
DON'T CLICK ON IT
(or you could get a horrible virus)
(like my grandmother did)

And if you upload the wrong thing, or post something you shouldn't, and it goes viral...you could destroy your whole life.

You might think I'm exaggerating. I'm not. I personally saw this happen just last month. And I decided to write this history as a warning to other kids about what NOT to do online. If you follow the "Internet Pro Tips" included at several points in this book, hopefully they'll save you from having to

learn a whole bunch of valuable lessons the
hard way.

like the one about viruses on p. 2

    Like my brother did.

REESE TAPPER, video game addict/soccer player/Internet disaster victim

    This was DEFS the craziest stuff
that ever happened to me. And it was so
fast! It's, like, one minute I was playing
MetaWorld, minding my own business, like,
"La-la-la, nothing going on..."

    And the next minute, "KA-BLOOM!"

    It was like getting launched into space
on a rocket. At first, it was awesome!

    But then the rocket exploded.

    That's the scary thing about the
Internet. You can get skronked ← *not a real word (Reese made it up) (he does this a lot) (it's v. annoying)*
into a million pieces without even
leaving your bedroom.

Reese = car

Internet = tree

MOM AND DAD (Text messages copied from Dad's phone)

MOM

Claudia's writing another oral history

= interviews with everybody involved

Oh geez. What's it about this time?

DAD

The whole Internet nightmare

I'm okay with that.

Srsly?????

Why not? Seems like good teachable moment

We'll look totally clueless about what our kids are doing online!

So what? All parents are clueless

I WORK AT A TECH COMPANY I'M NOT SUPPOSED TO BE CLUELESS ABOUT THIS STUFF

if you are reading this and work with my mom, SHE IS V. BRILLIANT BUSINESSPERSON WHO IS TOTALLY ON TOP OF EVERYTHING

Just make sure nobody you work with reads the book

CHAPTER 1
I MIGHT HAVE JUST WRITTEN
A HIT SONG

CLAUDIA

It all started when I wrote
a song. Then I posted it online.
Because I was hoping it would go
viral, and millions of people
would listen to it and turn it
into a massive hit.

REESE

Basically, you were trying
to get famous.

CLAUDIA

I guess so. But not in a gross way.
I'm not one of those people who's totally
into herself and desperate for attention,
so she vlogs every day on MeVid about
her shoes, or her nail polish, or how
her dog barfed in the car on the way
to the vet.

ANNA BANANAS: world's most annoying
MeVid vlogger (13,000,000 subscribers) (ugh!)
(+ ep where her dog barfed was DISGUSTING)

RING RING RING BANANAPHONE LOL!!

AnnaBananas   3,385,204 Views

For me, it's all about my music.
The only way I'd ever want to get
famous is by creating amazing songs (or getting
that people love. And I work VERY   elected president
of U.S.A.—
hard at it. I've been taking guitar   but that is a
lessons for almost three years, and   whole other
I try to practice an hour every day.   story) (which
you can read in
THE TAPPER TWINS
RUN FOR PRESIDENT)

REESE

You're for sure getting better. Like, I
used to hear you practice and think, "Is she
playing that guitar? Or just chewing on the
strings? 'Cause that does NOT sound like music."

But lately, I'm more like, "Hey, I think that's an actual song."

CLAUDIA   (sarcasm)

Thanks, Reese. I'm SO glad you don't think it sounds like I'm chewing on my guitar strings.

REESE

Not as glad as I am. My bedroom's right next to yours. And the walls are mad thin.

CLAUDIA

FYI, Reese and I live in New York City. Which is very inspiring, because a LOT of famous singer-songwriters have lived here. For example, John Lennon of the Beatles used to live just thirteen and a half blocks from our apartment on the Upper West Side.

THE DAKOTA: v. famous apt bldg where John Lennon used to live

our non-famous bldg is 13.5 blocks ←that way

And according to OMG Celebrities In The Wild!, my absolutely favorite singer-songwriter of all time, Miranda Fleet, just bought an apartment downtown for 20 million dollars. Which is completely crazy. It seems like if you spend 20 million dollars, you should get the whole building.

MIRANDA FLEET'S $20 MILLION APARTMENT

$5M living room? $3M kitchen? $2M guest bathroom?

Anyway, not only have I worked incredibly hard on my guitar skills, but I've been writing tons of songs lately. The one I posted online, "Windmill," was the tenth song I'd written just that week.

This is because whenever I have majorly intense feelings I don't know how to deal with, I write songs about them to try to get my head straight. And I was in serious emotional pain that whole week. I'm not going to discuss why, because it's personal and nobody's business.

SOPHIE KOH, best friend of Claudia

Claudia, you HAVE to discuss it! You're still hurting inside! You need to talk it out!

PARVATI GUPTA, second-best friend of Claudia

OMG, Claude, you TOTALLY have to! Not only that, you DEFS need to call out Jens for how insanely cruel he was to you.

CARMEN GUTIERREZ, other second-best friend of Claudia

Seriously. You're writing this book to teach people important lessons, right? Well, you know what's an incredibly important lesson that every boy on earth should learn?

"DON'T BREAK UP WITH SOMEBODY IN A TEXT MESSAGE!"

CLAUDIA

Okay, fine. I will discuss the breakup.
But just for a second.

PARVATI

More than that! Make it a whole chapter!

SOPHIE

Totally. It should be its own chapter.

CLAUDIA

Ugh! Fine.

CHAPTER 2
JENS KUYPERS
BROKE UP WITH ME
IN A TEXT MESSAGE

"Jens" is pronounced "Yens" (he is from the Netherlands) (where J's sound like Y's)

CLAUDIA

Jens Kuypers and I went out for about four months. And we had gotten pretty close. So I really thought I knew him as a person.

Which is why it was basically devastating when he randomly texted me on a Tuesday night and broke up with me.

RELATIONSHIP

~~INTERNET~~ PRO TIP:
NEVER BREAK UP WITH
SOMEONE IN A TEXT MESSAGE!

Since Jens has only lived in America for about six months, and his English still isn't great, at first I didn't really understand what he was saying.

JENS AND CLAUDIA (text messages)

No

Not ok

We need to talk NOW

Sorry really busy. Had soccer game earlier

I cant believe this

R u mad

CLAUDIA

For the record, "mad" does not really come close to describing how I felt. It was maybe 10% of my total feelings.

other 90% of feelings were:
-shocked
-betrayed
-confused
-sad
-barfy
-heartbroken
-MURDEROUSLY RAGEFUL

REESE

You were SO sad after that breakup! I felt so bad for you, I tried to get Mom and Dad to get a puppy to cheer you up.

CLAUDIA

You were just using my breakup as an

excuse! You've been trying to get Mom and
Dad to get us a puppy for YEARS.

REESE

    I know. But I still felt bad for you.

PARVATI

    Jens was just the worst. And I STILL
think you should get back at him by posting
that totally embarrassing pic on your
ClickChat page.

CLAUDIA

    I'd never do that. No matter how much he
deserves it. It's just too mean.

I WOULD NEVER POST THIS INCREDIBLY
EMBARRASSING PHOTO OF JENS ONLINE

CARMEN

On the bright side, though, you DID get an awesome song out of it.

CLAUDIA

Like I said, I wrote a lot of songs about the breakup. But "Windmill" was definitely the best. It had an awesome riff, and the chorus ("One day you're up and the next day you're down / Life is like a windmill going round and round...") was super catchy.

So I kind of suspected it was good. But I didn't realize HOW good until I played it for my guitar teacher, Randy.

FULL LIST OF BREAKUP SONGS I WROTE:
—Devastated
—It's Over
—Brown Eyes, Black Heart
—Deleted (aka The Swipe Left Song)
—Textless
—Jens Is a Yerk (WARNING: explicit lyrics)
—Empty Vest
—Brand New Me
—Windmill

RANDY RHOADS, Claudia's guitar teacher

I'm not jiving you, kid. "Windmill" is a HOT song.

Randy is from the 1970s

CLAUDIA

But you say that about all my songs.

RANDY THE GUITAR TEACHER
(he rocks!) (esp for someone his age)

RANDY

Well, yeah. But...I'm a guitar teacher. Being encouraging is half the gig. So even if some cat brings in a tune that makes me want to stab myself in the ear with a pencil, I gotta be all, "Great job, kiddo! Keep at it!"

CLAUDIA

Umm...this is actually kind of awkward. How many of MY songs have made you want to stab yourself in the ear with a pencil?

RANDY

Don't go there, kid. We're just talking "Windmill" right now. Which is HOT! No jive. That song could be on the radio.

CLAUDIA

After Randy told me it was great and helped me write a bridge for it, I played "Windmill" for my friends while we were all on a ClickChat video hangout.

bridge = part in mid-song that's different from the rest of the song

And they pretty much loved it.

SOPHIE

If that song came up on a playlist, I would DEFINITELY check to see who the artist was. And I would get ALL her songs.

PARVATI

OMG IT WAS THE MOST AMAZING SONG EVER!

I was like, "I can't believe this! You're going to be a star! And I'm going to be in your entourage! SQUEEEEEE!"

CLAUDIA

Until my friends heard it, I hadn't even been thinking about putting "Windmill" online. I knew for a fact that my idol, Miranda Fleet, didn't start putting songs out until she was fourteen. So I figured I should wait until I was at least in seventh grade.

But after I played it for them, all three of my friends told me I absolutely had to put it out there and get huge.

So I did.

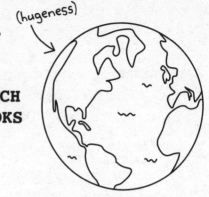

(me) →. (hugeness)

CHAPTER 3
GETTING HUGE IS MUCH
HARDER THAN IT LOOKS

CLAUDIA

The first thing I had to do was make a video. Because on the Internet, you can't just ask people to listen to a song—you have to give them something to look at while they're listening.

Carmen is very artistic, and she agreed to direct the video for me.

CARMEN

I've been wanting to get into filmmaking for a while. So this was a great opportunity. And it was kind of a challenge. Because you wouldn't let me show your face in the video.

CLAUDIA

I didn't want Carmen putting my face in the video because A) I wanted to keep the focus on the music, and B) sometimes when I play guitar, I scrunch up my eyes in a weird-looking way, and I didn't want people seeing that and trolling me for it.

REESE

It's hilarious when you make that guitar face! You look like you're pooping!

CLAUDIA

This is EXACTLY what I mean by "trolling."

Instead of filming me playing the song, Carmen shot close-ups of my hands playing the guitar. Then she intercut those with shots of a pinwheel that we filmed on the roof garden of my building.

STILL FRAME FROM "WINDMILL" MUSIC VIDEO

The video turned out great. And Carmen was totally right that a pinwheel was just as good as an actual windmill. So I'd like to officially apologize to her for the fight we got into about that.

CARMEN

It's all good. I mean, it's not like
I didn't WANT to use a real windmill. It's
just that it's basically impossible to find
them in New York City. And when you do, they
don't look like windmills.

ACTUAL NYC WINDMILLS (not very windmill-like)

CLAUDIA

After Carmen finished the "Windmill"
video and all I had to do was upload it to
MeVid, I got incredibly nervous. Because the
way my friends were talking, this video was
going to be MAJOR. And it seemed like once
I put it online, my whole life might change
forever.

CLICKCHAT POSTS (PRIVATE CHAT)

Carmen **c_2_the_g** can't wait for this vid to blow up 😁

Sophie **sophie_k_nyc** srsly. Its going to break the Internet

Parvati **Parvanana** U R GOING TO BE A STAR @claudaroo!!!
🕯️ 🕯️ 🕯️ 🐵

Parvanana U WILL TAKE ME ON TOUR W YOU RIGHT???
🕯️ 🐵 ✈️ ✈️

me **claudaroo** I dunno you guys. I'm kind of scared to post it

sophie_k_nyc But it's awesome! And u worked so hard on it!

You should post right now

c_2_the_g If u dont post it I will @claudaroo

Parvanana POST IT SO WE CAN GO MENTAL
😁 😁 😁 😁 😁

c_2_the_g u r already mental @Parvanana 😜 😜 😜

Parvanana TRUE. IM ABOUT TO PEE MYSELF
💧 💧 💧 💧

sophie_k_nyc Eeeeeeew

Parvanana JK

c_2_the_g Cmon @claudaroo post it!!!!!

CLAUDIA

It took me a whole day to get up the courage to put "Windmill" on MeVid. When I finally did, I posted on ClickChat to let everybody know about it:

claudaroo

♥ 24 likes

claudaroo Hey everybody! My new music video is up at http://mevid.com...I hope you like it! Thx to @c_2_the_g for doing an awesome job directing! And to @Parvanana and @sophie_k_nyc for all the support!

CLAUDIA

   Then I shut down my computer, because I didn't want to spend all night constantly reloading the MeVid page to see how many views I'd gotten.

   But I couldn't help myself. So after half an hour of pacing back and forth in my room and reminding myself to stay totally down-to-earth no matter how huge I got, I went back online.

Then I spent the rest of the night constantly reloading the MeVid page.

It turned out I didn't have to worry about staying down-to-earth. Or about my life changing forever. Or even for five minutes.

Because nobody watched the video. That whole first night it was online, it only got 37 views.

And at least 30 of those were Parvati.

Windmill (by Claudia Tapper)
claudaroo   37 Views

PARVATI

I had it on repeat. Because it was SO AWESOME!

CLAUDIA

By the next morning, "Windmill" was only up to 41 views. And I realized if I wanted to make it a hit, I was going to have to do a TON of promoting it.

Which felt a little icky. But fortunately, my friends helped a lot.

CARMEN

We pretty much forced the whole Culvert Prep sixth grade to watch it.

PARVATI

It wasn't just sixth graders. I was personally responsible for at LEAST ten page views from eighth graders.

AKASH GUPTA, eighth grader/older brother of Parvati

My annoying little sister parked her butt at our lunch table and refused to leave until my friends and I all watched Claudia's video on our phones.

PARVATI

Aren't you glad I did? You LOVE "Windmill"!

AKASH

It's pretty catchy. Not my kind of music, though. If there was an EDM remix, I'd be more into that.

CLAUDIA

The reaction I got from kids at school was VERY encouraging.

KALISHA HENDRICKS, sixth grader/extremely smart person

It's a really excellent song, Claudia. You should be proud of yourself.

DIMITRI SHARANSKY, sixth grader/moderately smart person

Big ups! It was cool.

CLAUDIA

Although not everybody was encouraging. The Fembots all ragged on it. Then again, they rag on everything.

FEMBOTS = annoying 6th grade rich girls who look down on everybody else for not being rich/annoying enough

ATHENA COHEN, Fembot dictator

I'm sorry, but that video was, like, TOTAL amateur hour. I mean, like, what was the budget for that? Like, five dollars?

CLAUDIA

It was actually more like zero dollars?
Because there was no budget at all?

ATHENA

Yeah, well, congratulations. It totally
shows.

BTW, all that begging you did to get
people to share it on ClickChat? Totally
classless. And SUCH a fail. What'd you get,
like, five views?

CLAUDIA

If you couldn't tell already, Athena
Cohen is evil.

Unfortunately, though, she was also
right. Even though almost all the kids at
Culvert Prep liked the video, there weren't
nearly enough of them to make it a viral
hit. Or any other kind of hit.

But it wasn't for lack of trying. I
reposted the link on ClickChat a bunch of
times, and I asked everybody I knew to share
and/or link to it. Including Mom and Dad,
even though they're not on ClickChat. And
Dad's barely even on Facebook.

MOM AND DAD (text messages)

Don't forget to post Claudia's video on your FB page

Already did. It got three likes!

That's it? How many FB friends do you have?

No idea

I checked. You have 23

Is that good?

It's terrible

Are you sure?

Yes. Makes me feel weird about being married to you

How many FB friends do you have?

632

OMG

There is no way all those people are
your friends

Reese has 786 on ClickChat

How is that even possible????

Reese has not met 786 people in his
whole life!!!

When you get home, I will explain
how social media works

Not sure I want to know

CLAUDIA

At one point, Carmen told me to add
hashtags to the MeVid page so people could
find "Windmill" in search. So I did.

Windmill (by Claudia Tapper)

claudaroo #Songs #Songwriters #Music   **198 Views**
#Windmill

CARMEN

You barely tagged it! I was like, "Claude—do I have to do this for you?"

CLAUDIA

Carmen insisted on redoing my hashtags. Tbh, I think she went a little overboard.

Windmill (by Claudia Tapper)

claudaroo #Songs #Songwriters #SingerSongwriters #SongwriterSingers #NYCSongwriters #NYCSongs #Hits #HitSongs #SongHits #BestSongs #GreatestSongs #GSOAT #Music #GoodMusic #GreatMusic #AwesomeMusic #AmazingMusic #Video #MusicVideo #GreatMusicVideo #Breakup #BreakupSongs #SongsAboutBreakups #SongsAboutBreakingUp #BreakingUpSongs #Heartache #Heartbreak #Sad #Bittersweet #MovingOn #GirlPower #Girls #Sisters #StrongSisters #SistersAreDoinIt #BoysSuck #Claudia #ClaudiaTapper #TapperClaudia #Carmen #CarmenGutierrez #CarmenGutierrezDirector #CarmenDirects #Windmill #Windmills #SongsAboutWindmills #Pinwheel #PinwheelVsWindmill #WindmillVsPinwheel #CanAPinwheelBeAWindmill #Rooftop #RooftopVideo #VideoRooftop #VideosOnRooftops #NYC #NYCRooftop #RooftopNYC #NYCRooftopMusicVideoWithPinwheelInIt

214 Views

CARMEN

You can NEVER have too many hashtags.

CLAUDIA

I'm not sure that's true.

Anyway, the hashtags were not exactly a game changer. And neither were all my ClickChat posts. After a week online, "Windmill" was stuck around 300 page views, and it looked like it was never going to take off.

(1 week after posting)

Windmill (by Claudia Tapper)

claudaroo #Songs #Songwriters
#SingerSongwriters #SongwriterSingers
293 Views

So I got desperate and did what Parvati had been begging me to do all along: I Blurted it.

CHAPTER 4
BLURT—THE WORST/BEST SITE
ON THE INTERNET

CLAUDIA

In case you're like my parents and have no clue what Blurt is, it's a "microvideo" social network. The only things you can post on it are two-second videos.

"microvlog"? (not sure)

Depending on who you talk to, this makes Blurt either insanely cool or totally ridiculous. For example, I think it's ridiculous. Because pretty much nothing fits into a two-second video except things that are completely stupid—like riding your bike into a swimming pool or pulling your pants down at a McDonald's.

shadowtal

2,385,233 BLIPS

YUNG T JOINS #HALLOFMEAT!!!!

REESE

Blurt is AWESOME! It's a whole site of nothing but dudes riding their bikes into swimming pools and pulling their pants down at McDonald's!

It's off the hook hilarious.

SOPHIE

Blurt is officially the dumbest thing in the history of the universe.

PARVATI

I LOVE IT!!!

Seriously. If it weren't for Blurt, I wouldn't know who Tyler Purdy is! Or Marcel Mourlot, Austin Flick, Luke Vivian, Cody and Cody, Jimmy Wallinger, Oscar Gonzalez, or Brian Messer!

CLAUDIA

Parvati has crushes on about twenty different Blurt stars. Which I do not really get. I mean, some of them are definitely cute. But they don't DO anything. Most of their Blurts are just them making dumb jokes or staring into the camera and going, "HEEEEEEY BAAAAAAE..."

PARVATI

Okay, first of all—Tyler Purdy doesn't HAVE to do anything except stare into the camera. HIS EYES ARE SOOOOO BLUE! I could seriously watch Blurts of Tyler's eyes for WEEKS.

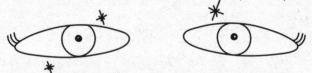

TYLER PURDY'S EYES (Dad says I can't use actual pic without written permission from Tyler's eyes)

Second, it's not true that none of them do anything. Marcel Mourlot's inspirational Blurts are helping millions of people live their best possible life!

And Brian Messer's a huge pop star. AND he got his start on Blurt! Just like you should!

CLAUDIA

I personally am not a big fan of Brian Messer's music. But it's true he's gotten pretty huge. AND it all started with him posting tons of Blurts with little 2-second clips of his songs and a link so you could listen to the whole song on MeVid if you liked it.

I always thought this was crazy, because how can you tell if you like a song in two seconds? But after a week of watching "Windmill" go nowhere online, I finally took Parvati's advice and started Blurting clips from it.

claudaroo   634 BLIPS

WINDMILL pt. 1 (by Claudia Tapper)

I posted about thirty Blurts in total.
I would've done more, but it's pretty hard to
cut a song into two-second clips that make
any kind of sense.

PARVATI

They're not SUPPOSED to make sense! I
feel like you're missing the whole point of
Blurt.

CLAUDIA

That's probably true.

Anyway, I not only hashtagged all the
clips, but Parvati had me tag a bunch of
famous Blurters in the comments so it'd show
up in their notifications, and they'd hopefully
Reblurt me. Reblurt = when you share somebody
else's Blurt on your Blurt page

@claudaroo @TheRealMarcel @BrianMesser @CodyAndCody
@PurdyTyler @FlicknAusome

None of them did. Even so, at first I
thought my Blurt numbers looked pretty good.
My most popular Blurt had 2,236 Blips in its
first week.

Blip = 1 view of a Blurt

2,236 BLIPS

my biggest Blurt
(from mid-chorus)
("like a Windmill
going round and")

But since Blurts are only two seconds,
and they play on a loop, it turns out 2,236
Blips is actually not much at all. You
can practically get 1,000 Blips just by
accident.

PARVATI

I left one of your Blurts running while
I went to the bathroom, and I think that was
good for about 500 Blips. Maybe more.

CLAUDIA

After all the Blurting I did, I wound
up with a couple hundred Blurt followers.
But I think they were mostly bots.
And even if they were actual
humans, not too many of them
watched the full video. Even after two
weeks of full-time Blurting, "Windmill"
still had less than 400 views on MeVid.

"bots" =
robot accounts
that follow you but
aren't actual humans

"Windmill"
MeVid views

388 Views

<< 37 >>

| claudaroo | (208) FOLLOWERS | 116 FOLLOWING |

my Blurt followers

I was pretty bummed about that. It was a great song, and almost everybody who heard it loved it. But no matter how hard I tried, I couldn't get people to click on it.

Not only did it NOT go viral, it didn't even come close.

So I decided that getting huge on the Internet was basically impossible.

At least, I thought it was.

Until my brother did it without even trying.

CHAPTER 5
REESE GETS HIS BLURT ON

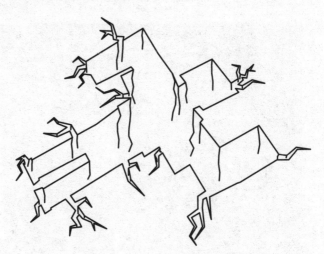

REESE

It all started with me and Xander
messing around on MetaWorld. MetaWorld =
video game where Reese
Version 3.0 just came out, spends 80% of his life
and they added this thing (other 20% = soccer)
called a "physics engine." Which makes
stuff look WAY more realistic. Even though
everybody's still got, like, square heads
and no fingers.

So when Xander threw me off a cliff
during a deathmatch, instead of just dying
like in 2.0, my avatar went "SPLAAAAM!" and
made this awesome-looking avatar-shaped hole
in the ground.

It was hilarious! So Xander and I
started jumping off cliffs just for fun.

71346 MK/23100293 GZ
00:34:11

avatar-shaped hole in the
ground (prob Xander?)

H1z KillN11

Skronkmonster

Reese's
avatar

CLAUDIA

    FYI, Xander Billington is one of Reese's
best friends. He's also incredibly annoying.

**XANDER BILLINGTON, friend of Reese/
incredibly annoying person**

    Don't start no beef with me, Clownia!
You step to the X-Man, I'ma bring da
ruckus to yo' door!

Xander's
nickname
for me

Xander's nickname
for himself

CLAUDIA

One of the many annoying things about Xander is that he constantly talks like he's in a rap battle. Which is especially sad when you consider that his ancestors were some of the original Pilgrims who came over from England on the *Mayflower*.

This means the Billingtons have officially been the most annoying family in America for almost 400 straight years.

THE LANDING OF THE PILGRIMS AT PLYMOUTH, MASS. DEC. 22ND 1620.

XANDER

No way, dawg! Dem Billingtons got MAD respect back in the day!

CLAUDIA

Xander, have you ever googled "*Mayflower*" and "Billingtons"? Because I did. And it turns out one of your ancestors almost blew up the ship. And another one got hanged for murder after they landed in America.

100% TRUE (you can google this)

XANDER

WUUUUT?? No way that's legit.

CLAUDIA

It is completely legit.

XANDER

Straight up? No frontin'?

CLAUDIA

Straight up. No fronting. Dawg.

XANDER

AWWWW, YEAH!! THAT'S HOW WE DO! BILLINGTONS IS O.G., YO!!! I can't wait to tell Mom-a-saurus 'bout this at dinner tonight. She gonna be all, "BODY COUNT! Raise da roof!"

CLAUDIA

I'm getting seriously off track here.
Back to MetaWorld.

REESE

Jumping off cliffs got boring after
a while. But then I was like, "What if we
build a giant tower and jump off that?"

So we did. And it was awesome!
Especially when we tricked Wyatt into
standing in front of the tower so we could
crush him when we landed.

WYATT TEMPLEMAN, friend of Reese

The first time they did that, I got really mad. Because they didn't tell me what they were going to do. But then they let ME jump on THEM for a while. And it was SO funny! I was dying.

REESE'S AVATAR (IN MID-JUMP)

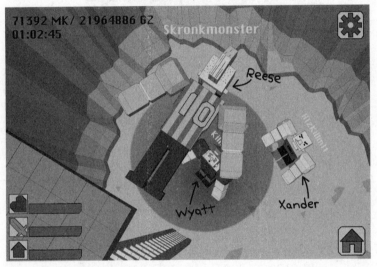

XANDER

Then I was all, "Yo, we should straight-up Blurt this!"

REESE

It was a perfect clip for Blurt. 'Cause it took, like, EXACTLY two seconds to jump

off the tower and splat somebody's avatar.
So Xander took a video of me jumping onto
Wyatt. Then I posted it.

CLAUDIA

I will admit that even though it's
not my kind of humor, the first time I saw
Reese's Blurt, I laughed out loud. It was
one of those involuntary-laugh situations.
Like when you're watching a movie and a cute
little girl kicks a big huge guy in the
crotch. You don't WANT to laugh. But you do.

(REESE'S BLURT)

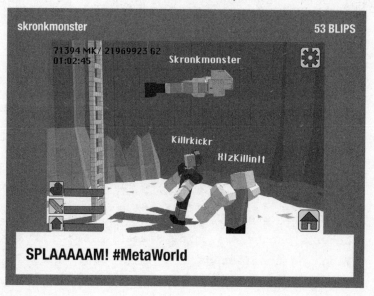

REESE

I'd never posted anything on Blurt before. I'd just watched stuff. So I didn't have any Blurt followers except Xander and Wyatt. And by the time Mom got home that night and made me turn off my computer, my Blurt only had, like, 50 Blips.

But then Xander tagged a bunch of our friends in the comments to get them to check it out.

@XlzKillinIt **CHECK IT** @numbah_tehn @Wenzamura @nightstaker @bryce_thompson @shabado02 @AidanTheGrif

So when I got up the next morning and checked Blurt, I had 600 Blips! And 10 new followers!

And when I got to the cafeteria before school started, practically the whole sixth grade was watching it.

CLAUDIA

Kids were all crowding around each other's phones, watching Reese's Blurt and laughing their heads off.

And I am going to be completely honest:
it was annoying to me.

Because everybody was MUCH more
excited about some two-second thing Reese
had put zero thought into than they ever
were about "Windmill." Which I had not only
spent WEEKS trying to get people to listen
to...but actually took me YEARS of hard work,
if you count all the time I spent getting
better at guitar and learning how to write
songs before I could come up with something
really good.

It just did not seem fair at all.

But I never, EVER would've made a big
deal about it if stupid Athena Cohen hadn't
opened her mouth.

CHAPTER 6
NEVER GAMBLE
WITH A FEMBOT

CLAUDIA

Athena rules the Fembots by fear. She tries to rule the rest of the sixth grade that way, too, but most kids don't buy into it. Although enough of them do that Athena THINKS she rules the whole grade.

Fembots are:
—Athena
—Clarissa Parker
—Ling Chen
—Meredith Timms
+ 5–8 wannabes

And she can smell weakness like a shark can smell blood. Whenever somebody's feeling sad, or small, or spun out, Athena notices. Then she attacks them.

This is pretty much what she did to me in the cafeteria that morning.

ATHENA SELFIE
(jk)

SOPHIE

You were just sitting there, minding your own business. And all of a sudden, Athena was like, "EVERYBODY LOOK AT CLAUDIA! SHE'S SOOOO UPSET!"

CLAUDIA

For the record, I was NOT "upset" about how much attention Reese's Blurt was getting. I was "annoyed." Which is totally different.

But when Athena yelled that, everybody stopped watching the Blurt and started watching ME. And Athena said something like, "You BEGGED people for WEEKS to watch your lame video...and in five seconds, Reese made something A HUNDRED TIMES as popular! AHAHAHAHAHA!"

Which was ridiculous. Because my most popular Blurt had gotten over 2,000 Blips. And at that point, Reese's MetaWorld Blurt still only had 600.

647 BLIPS

REESE

It was actually more like 1,000 by then. It was going up pretty fast.

CLAUDIA

Whatever. The point is, I was NOT upset...until Athena tried to humiliate me in front of everybody. And even then I didn't get upset. I got ANGRY.

I actually got so angry I couldn't think straight. So instead of just laughing at Athena—which is what I SHOULD have done—I took the bait. I can't remember exactly what I said—

SOPHIE

It was something like, "Oh, please! My songs are going to be around a LOT longer than Reese's stupid Blurt."

CLAUDIA

I definitely should not have said that. Because I wasn't even mad at Reese! I was mad at Athena! But then it somehow turned into this whole me-against-my-brother situation, and EVERYBODY got involved— the Fembots, Reese's friends, my friends— everybody.

CARMEN

We were trying to stick up for you!

That's the only reason Parvati mentioned
Blurt followers.

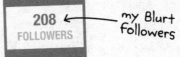

208
FOLLOWERS

my Blurt followers

PARVATI

I was like, "Claudia's got two hundred
Blurt followers, and Reese only has ten!
That makes her two hundred times more
popular than him!"

I got the math wrong, but whatever.

REESE

I didn't even want to get involved.
But when Parvati was all, "You only have
ten followers!" I said, "No way!
I got twenty! That's, like, ten
more than I had an hour ago!"

23
FOLLOWERS

Reese

SOPHIE

(Fembot vice-dictator)

Then Clarissa Parker was all, "I'd bet
a thousand dollars Reese ends up with more
followers than Claudia."

And Athena heard that and just ran
with it.

CLAUDIA

Before I knew it, Athena was all up in
my face, sticking her hand out and going,

"Bet me! A thousand dollars! Or do you want to just admit you're a LOSER?"

EVERYBODY was watching us. And all I could think was, "There is NO WAY I am letting Athena bully me in front of everybody."

But I also didn't have a thousand dollars. I didn't even have ten dollars.

Mom + Dad don't give me or Reese allowance, which is v. unfair

CARMEN

Of course not! Nobody has that kind of money except Athena. But your comeback was SO great.

CLAUDIA

I can't remember my exact words. But they were something like, "I'm sorry, Athena. I'm just not rich and spoiled enough to waste a thousand dollars of my daddy's money on a totally pointless bet. And if I DID have a thousand dollars? I'd use it to make the world a better place. I wouldn't throw it in people's faces like you do."

REESE

Athena was ripped when you said that. People were all, "WHOOOO! BURRRRN!"

Reese actually v. supportive of me against Athena, which was cool of him

CLAUDIA

Then Athena said something like, "My bad—I TOTALLY forgot you're poor!" But nobody laughed except a couple of Fembots.

After that, she was quiet for a second. But you could practically see the evil little wheels turning in her evil little brain.

And then she said, "Fine. You don't have to bet a dime. If you win, I'll give you a thousand dollars to make your little world a better place.

"But if I win...you have to post a Blurt saying, 'I'M CLAUDIA TAPPER, AND I'M THE LAMEST, STUPIDEST, MOST BASIC [PERSON] WHO EVER LIVED.'"

had to edit this b/c Athena's language was NOT appropriate

REESE

Everybody was like, "YEAH! DO IT, CLAUDIA! TAKE THE BET!"

I was cheering for it, and I couldn't even remember what the bet was.

CLAUDIA

At that point, I couldn't remember what it was, either. I just knew I couldn't let Athena win.

SOPHIE

You were like, "What are we even betting on here?" And Athena said, "Whether Reese ends up with more Blurt followers than you."

Then you guys argued for a while about how long the bet should last, and what the rules should be, and stuff like that.

And then before you shook on it, Athena made Toby type the whole thing up.

CLAUDIA

Here is the exact bet that Toby Zimmerman sent to everybody right after Athena and I shook hands on it in front of the whole sixth grade:

THE BET
ATHENA BETS CLAUDIA THAT BY THE TIME SCHOOL ENDS AT 2:55PM ON THURSDAY THE 26TH, REESE (@SKRONKMONSTER) WILL HAVE MORE BLURT FOLLOWERS THAN CLAUDIA (@CLAUDAROO).

THE STAKES
IF CLAUDIA HAS MORE FOLLOWERS, ATHENA WILL PAY CLAUDIA $1,000.

IF REESE HAS MORE FOLLOWERS, CLAUDIA WILL POST A BLURT ON HER @CLAUDAROO ACCOUNT OF HERSELF SAYING "I'M CLAUDIA TAPPER, AND I'M THE LAMEST, STUPIDEST, MOST BASIC IDIOT WHO EVER LIVED".

RULES
REESE CAN'T CHEAT OR SET HIS ACCOUNT TO PRIVATE OR DO ANYTHING ELSE TO HELP HIS SISTER WIN OR SHE WILL AUTOMATICALLY LOSE.

IF ANYBODY CREATES FAKE BLURT ACCOUNTS JUST TO FOLLOW PEOPLE, THEIR SIDE WILL AUTOMATICALLY LOSE.

IF CLAUDIA LOSES, IN HER BLURT SHE CAN'T WEAR SUNGLASSES OR MASKS OR ANYTHING TO HIDE HER FACE.

SHE ALSO CAN'T DELETE THE BLURT EVER.

CLAUDIA

It's very important to understand that when I made that bet with Athena, it did NOT seem like the dumbest thing I'd ever done in my life.

REESE

It totally didn't! 'Cause it was me against you—except I wanted you to win! So even though I had to swear I wouldn't help you, it's not like I was going to help Athena.

CLAUDIA

Also, when Athena and I shook hands on it in front of everybody, I was CRUSHING Reese in Blurt followers. I had 208. And Reese only had 23.

REESE

Right! So it didn't seem like the dumbest thing you'd ever done until at least a couple hours later.

CHAPTER 7
REESE GOES VIRAL

10,000,234 BLIPS

CLAUDIA

In math class, Ms. Santiago taught us about something called "exponential growth." Basically, when something grows exponentially, at first it seems like it's only growing KIND OF fast...then it starts growing REALLY fast...and then it basically skyrockets into outer space.

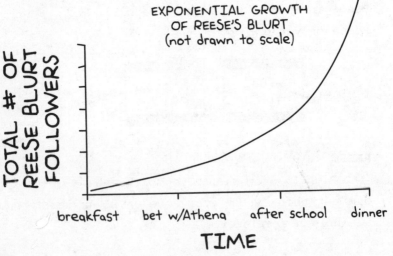

EXPONENTIAL GROWTH
OF REESE'S BLURT
(not drawn to scale)

TOTAL # OF REESE BLURT FOLLOWERS

breakfast   bet w/Athena   after school   dinner

TIME

This is pretty much what happened with
Reese's Blurt. By noon that day, he was up
to 5,000 Blips and 45 followers.

Which was a LOT more than he'd had when
I made the bet with Athena. So the Fembots
taunted me about it all through lunch.

SOPHIE

They were SO annoying. Ling Chen made up
some song like, "You're soooo dooooooomed...." ←
And then all the Fembots *to the tune of "You're So Vain"*
kept singing it over and over. *(which I'd never heard before)*
(it's not a bad song)
(except now it reminds
me of Fembots)
(so I hate it)

REESE

All my friends at lunch were like,
"Dude, you're blowing up!"

And Xander was all, "Half dem followers
iz MINE, yo!"

XANDER

I wuz ROBBED! You done recorded that
clip from MY account, yo! You couldn'ta done
it without me!

WYATT

What about me? It was my avatar Reese jumped on!

XANDER ← Xander's nickname for Wyatt

Step off, Y-Train. You wuz just meat. We coulda Hulk-smashed any fool.

REESE

I felt like Xander had a point. I mean, we'd built the whole tower together. And I couldn't have made the Blurt without him.

But it's not like you can just give somebody half your followers. So instead, I told him if he wanted, we could be a team. And the next time we did a Blurt, we'd post it from his account, so he'd get followers, too.

Plus, if I didn't post any more stuff on my own account, it'd be easier for you to win the bet.   (that is, me)
                                                    (Claudia)

CLAUDIA

I was hoping Reese's numbers would tail off after lunch, but the opposite happened. By the time school ended, he was up to 8,000 Blips and 65 followers.

Which was terrifying.

REESE

On the bus home, you were like, "Reese, you HAVE to stop people from following you!"

M79 BUS CROSSING CENTRAL PARK (was here when I begged Reese to stop people from following him)

But I was like, "I can't! If I set my account to private, Athena will see it and you'll automatically lose!" And there was basically no other way to stop people from following me.

Besides, I was psyched. I was getting Reblurts every minute! From people I didn't even know!

CLAUDIA

Reese was 10% worried for me that I'd lose the bet with Athena and 90% thrilled that his Blurt was getting so much attention.

And I was 10% happy for him, 5% annoyed that something so stupid was that popular, and 85% FREAKING THE HECK OUT that I was going to lose the bet and have to post a completely humiliating Blurt of myself.

It already seemed like there was a very good chance Reese would end up with more than 208 followers. Which meant I was going to have to do a LOT more Blurting to boost my followers.

So as soon as I got home, I asked our after-school sitter, Ashley, to help me decide which of my songs I should release as a follow-up to "Windmill."

Ashley majored in Musical Theater when she was in college, which is why she was an excellent person to ask for musical advice. It's also why she's still our after-school sitter even though she's twenty-five years old and has a college degree.

ASHLEY O'ROURKE, after-school sitter

Claude, can you do me a solid and write in your book that if anybody who reads it is a theater, film, TV, or webisode producer, they should check out my reel on MeVid and/or come to my upcoming showcase at the People's Republic of Dance in Chelsea?

CLAUDIA

Absolutely, Ash. You're going to be a star someday! Your one-woman show was AMAZING.

Ashley backstage at her one-woman show, Cathedrals In My Brain

ASHLEY

Thanks, Claude! Also, please tell
people I'm available mornings and weekends
for babysitting. I'm good with all ages!
Especially babies. I'm like a ninja at
getting them to nap.

CLAUDIA

Back to the story: I was in my bedroom
with Ashley, playing one of my songs "Deleted
for her, when we heard the screams (aka The
Swipe Left
coming from Reese's room. Song)"

REESE

BewBewBoy's the most famous MetaWorlder
ever. I've been watching his videos since
I was ten. He's got, like, thirty million
followers on MeVid. And twenty million on
Blurt.

AND HE REBLURTED ME!!! TO TWENTY MILLION
PEOPLE!!!

And THAT'S when everything went insta-
cray.

ASHLEY

Reese was screaming so loud, I thought
he'd chopped his finger off or something.

And as his caregiver, that DEFINITELY
would've been on me.

So I ran to his bedroom. And it turned
out he was screaming because he'd just
gotten 100,000 Blips in ten seconds.

114,692 BLIPS

CLAUDIA

I'm not personally responsible if Reese
chops his fingers off, so I was a little
slower to get up than Ashley was. And in
the five extra seconds it took me to get to
Reese's room, he got another 50,000 Blips.

He was staring at the Blip counter on
his page and screaming "THIS IS AMAZING!"
and "AAAAAAAHHH!!!" over and over again.

168,006 BLIPS

REESE

It was NUTS!!!! I was getting, like,
ten thousand Blips a second!

379,303 BLIPS

CLAUDIA

He was also getting a couple of new
followers every second. Which, if you do
the math, meant that every two minutes, he
was adding as many followers as I had in my
whole account.

I was not actually doing the math just

then. Because I was too busy having a panic
attack on the living room couch.

At least, I think it was a panic attack.
My heart was going "THUMP-THUMP-THUMP-
THUMP-THUMP," and I couldn't breathe, and I
thought I was going to pass out.

ASHLEY

The whole situation was super stressful.
I was trying to get you to lie on the couch
and breathe into a paper bag, AND I was
trying to get Reese to quit screaming, AND
I was trying to make dinner and fold the
laundry.   *Ashley not good at multi-tasking*

CLAUDIA

The paper bag was very helpful. But
only because it was SO TOTALLY USELESS that

I used my phone
to google "paper
bag breathe panic
attack" so I could
try to figure out
why anybody would
EVER think that'd be
helpful.

TOTALLY USELESS IN A PANIC ATTACK

And reading about panic attacks online distracted me from my actual panic attack long enough that I eventually settled down.

Reese, however, did NOT settle down. He pretty much only stopped screaming long enough to text Mom and Dad when he hit 1,000,000 Blips.

1,003,211 BLIPS

REESE AND MOM/DAD (Text messages copied from Reese's phone)

ZOMG BEWBEWBOY RBD ME N I GOT A MILLION BLIPS!!!

THIS IS CRAY!!!

D That's great, buddy!

D Now tell us what it means

I BLURTED A CLIP AND ITS BLOWING UP HUGE!!!

M How long have you had a Blurt account?

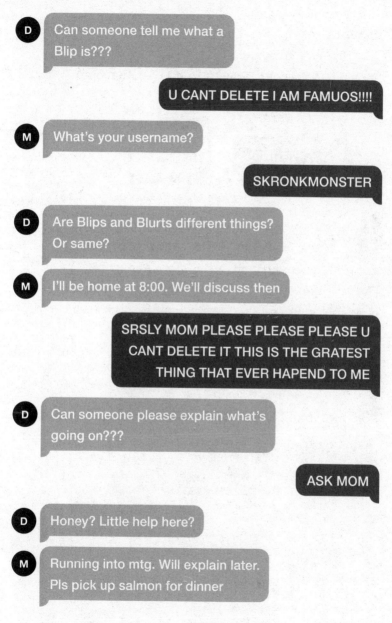

CLAUDIA

By the time Mom got home from work, Reese had almost 5,000,000 Blips and over 5,000 followers.

Which was so huge that Mom couldn't bring herself to make Reese delete his account even though he'd lied about his age to create it. (Which, tbh, pretty much everybody does. So if you ask me, Mom was overreacting.)

But she did get herself a Blurt account so she could keep an eye on us.

MOM AND DAD (text messages)

This is completely insane. Reese has 5M Blips! http://www.blurt.com...

Still no idea what that is

Click the link

It says I need to register

Can I use your login?

Seriously, Eric?

Just come home and watch it here

I am starving and both kids have lost their minds. Claudia in tears about some kind of bet and Reese won't stop running around screaming

REESE

I was crazy amped. I couldn't even sleep that night. 'Cause I was FAMOUS!

CLAUDIA

I couldn't sleep, either. 'Cause I was DOOMED. At the rate my "Windmill" Blurts had gotten me followers, if I wanted to catch up to Reese, I was going to have to write, record, and shoot videos for 1,000 songs.

And by the next morning, it was more like 2,000 songs.

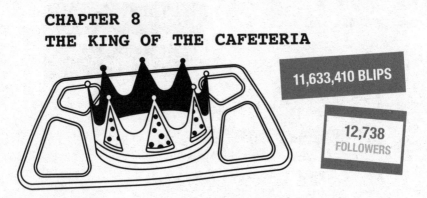

11,633,410 BLIPS

12,738
FOLLOWERS

CLAUDIA

By the time he walked into school on
Friday morning, Reese had over 10,000,000
Blips and 12,000 Blurt followers. And the
whole middle school was drooling over him
like he was some kind of actual celebrity.

Hunter and Bryce practically tackled him
on the way in. They were going, "Have you
hung out with BewBewBoy?" And, "What's he
like in person?"

Which was ridiculous. Because all
BewBewBoy had done was Reblurt Reese. And
he lives in Finland.

Then Natasha Minello ran up and asked
Reese if he could get Austin Flick's phone
number for her. Which was even MORE ridiculous.
Because even though Austin Flick had Reblurted
him, Reese had no clue who he even was.

tons of Blurt
stars RB'd
Reese after
BewBewBoy

REESE

When I got to the cafeteria, a bunch of girls were like, "Are you going to BlurtUp? Can you hook us up with Joey and Joey?" ~should be "Cody and Cody" (Reese even more clueless than me re Blurt stars)~

And I was like, "I do NOT know what you're talking about."

But then Xander was all, "HECKS TO THE YEAH, WE GOIN' TO DAT BLURTUP! WE GONNA BE MAIN STAGE, LADIES!!!"

CLAUDIA

BlurtUp is like a music festival, except with Blurt stars instead of rock stars. It was happening a week from that Saturday in the parking lot at Citi Field.

I knew this because it was all Parvati had been talking about for WEEKS.

CITI FIELD PARKING LOT (site of BlurtUp)
(so try to imagine it full of screaming teenage girls instead of cars/Mets fans)

PARVATI

OMG, ALL my fave Blurters were going to be there! Tyler, Marcel, Austin, Luke, Jimmy, Gina G, Wasted Wendy, Cody and Cody—

CLAUDIA

And Reese and Xander!

Except not. Because even though Xander told all the girls in the cafeteria he and Reese were going to be at BlurtUp, the only way that was going to happen was if they bought a ticket. Reese's 12,000 followers might be a ton for Culvert Prep, but it was still basically nothing compared to the millions of followers that actual Blurt stars have.

And Xander had no followers.

Literally, none. Not even Reese was following him.

XANDER

Cuz I'd just relaunched, yo! To hype dat Skronkmonsta brand!

REESE

My screen name's always been "Skronkmonster." Not just on Blurt, but

everywhere. And Xander's always been
"XIzKillinIt."

But after we decided to be a team, and
my Blurt got 10,000,000 Blips, Xander changed
HIS Blurt name to "Skronkmonster _ X."

Skronkmonster_X	0 FOLLOWERS	54 FOLLOWING

He got pretty ripped when Akash asked
him if that meant we were married.

AKASH

I said, "So, if you're taking Reese's
name...are you also planning to stay
home full time with the little baby
Skronkmonsters?"

XANDER

Not funny, yo. NOT. FUNNY.

AKASH

Actually, it was. I seem to recall a
cafeteria full of people laughing at you.

(Akash also not a fan of Xander)

CLAUDIA

For the record, when Reese had told me on the way to school that he and Xander were going to team up and try to become Blurt stars like BewBewBoy or Cody and Cody, I warned him it was a terrible idea. And not just because it meant he'd be breaking his promise not to post any more Blurts until my bet with Athena was over.

REESE

I HAD to keep posting! 'Cause, like, no offense? But there was no way you were going to win that bet. And now that I'd blown up huge, Xander had all these ideas for how we were going to turn pro and make a ton of money doing Blurts!

CLAUDIA

Like what ideas?

REESE

Well, he didn't have them YET. It's more like he had ideas for ideas.

And it was totally possible! BewBewBoy makes a million dollars a week! *not true (b/c BewBewBoy is Finnish) (so he makes a million euros) (not dollars)*

AKASH

BewBewBoy actually does rake a ton of cash. But mostly on MeVid. Because Blurt doesn't have advertising—so the only thing 10,000,000 Blips gets you is bragging rights. To turn the Blips into money, you have to be smart.

And that pretty much disqualified Xander and your brother.

CLAUDIA

While Reese was getting drooled over by half the school and dreaming about becoming a professional Blurter, I was hiding out in the school library to avoid the Fembots. Specifically, I was in the reference aisle. It's a perfect place to hide out because nobody ever goes there.

PARVATI

I didn't even know the reference aisle existed. It's, like, this secret part of the library. Like Narnia.

REFERENCE AISLE (aka library Narnia)

CLAUDIA

The reference aisle is also far enough
from Mr. Finch's spot at the circulation
desk that Parvati, Sophie, and I could talk
quietly without getting in trouble. And I
desperately needed to talk through how I was
going to get out of my bet with Athena.

I'd decided Reese was right—there was
no way I could win. But since the whole
sixth grade had watched me make the bet, I
also couldn't back out of it without major
humiliation.

And that'd not only be incredibly
embarrassing, it might even destroy my
political career. (I am 6th grade class president)
(For totally insane election story,
check out THE TAPPER TWINS
RUN FOR PRESIDENT)

SOPHIE

I could definitely see people making it
an issue in your re-election campaign.

But posting a Blurt where you call
yourself lame and stupid would ALSO be a
campaign issue.

CLAUDIA

I thought I might be able to find a
loophole in the contract. Like if I recorded
myself saying, "I'M THE LAMEST, STUPIDEST..."

etc., while standing on the sidewalk next to a jackhammer so nobody could hear the words.

SOPHIE

Bad idea. Campaign issue.

PARVATI

I thought you were giving up WAY too easily. You're an AMAZING singer-songwriter! And you had two whole weeks to become a Blurt star!

It's like Marcel Mourlot says: "Eef zhou can dream eet, zhou can BE EET!" *(Parvati imitating Marcel's French accent)*

MARCEL MOURLOT'S BIGGEST BLURT

TheRealMarcel   574,832,275 BLIPS

IF YOU CAN DREAM IT...YOU CAN BE IT!!!!!!!!!!

You just had to do what Reese did—get a
famous Blurter to Reblurt you! Like Marcel!
He has thirty million followers! AND he was
going to be at BlurtUp!

All you had to do was go to BlurtUp,
meet Marcel, and ask him to Reblurt you! It
was a total no-brainer.

CLAUDIA

It was NOT a no-brainer. Because when I
went online to look for tickets, I found out
the only way to actually meet any of the Blurt
stars in person was to buy a "VIP Platinum"
ticket with a "Meet and Greet" option. Which
cost $500. Which I DEFINITELY DID NOT HAVE.
And even if I did, they were sold out.

PARVATI

I just had a regular $30 ticket myself.
But I'd decided I was going to camp out
overnight and be the first person in line.
So when Tyler Purdy flew overhead in his
helicopter, he'd see me and realize I was
his absolutely biggest fangirl ever. And
he'd pull me out of the line and take
me backstage and feed me strawberries
for lunch.

SOPHIE

How did you know he was coming by helicopter?

PARVATI

I didn't. I also wasn't sure about the strawberries. But that's how I wrote it in my fanfic. And "EEF ZHOU CAN DREAM EEET, ZHOU CAN BE EET!" ← FANFIC = fan fiction = made-up stories about non-made-up people (and/or characters in books/movies/TV)

EXCERPT FROM PARVATI'S TYLER PURDY FANFIC

We Werent Supposed To Fall In Love   © Parvati Gupta   p.4

through the backstage area. There are a bunch of fancy couches and TVs with every kind of gaming console imaginable. As we go over to a huge blue couch we pass Austin Flick. Hes playing Xbox.

"Wut up bruh?" Tyler says.

"Oh hey."

"This is Parvati. We just met."

"Hey Parvati," says Austin. "It's awesome to meet you."

"You too," I say, like its n.b.d. I don't want to seem to uncool.

We sit down on a giant blue couch. The cushions are so comfy I could fall asleep on them forever.

"Your eyes are amazing," Tyler says. "When I saw them from the helicopter, I knew I had to meet you! I want to know everything about you. What's your favorite color?"

"Blue," I say. "The same color blue as your eyes."

"I can't believe it!" he says. "That's my favorite color too! Do you like strawberries?"

"I LOVE strawberries," I tell him. Because I really do. "They are like my favorite fruit ever."

"Wow this is crazy," says Tyler. "I think we might be soul mates." He takes out his phone. It has a sparkle case.

"Ohmygosh we have the exact same case!" I pull out my phone and show him.

"This is just too crazy," he says. "What's your username?"

I tell him its @parvanana. He has trouble spelling it so I take his phone and type it into Clickchat for him. When I give it back to him our fingers touch for a second. It feels like an electric shock only not painful.

"Cool" he says. "Now I'm following you. Oh hey check it out—a bunch of my followers just started following you too!"

I look at his phone. In five seconds I have gotten seven hundred thousands of

CLAUDIA

We didn't exactly solve my problem in the library that morning. And even though I waited until the last possible second to go to my locker, when I came down the hall, Athena and the Fembots were waiting for me like vultures.

When they saw me, they all started singing, "YOU'RE SOOO DOOOMED...!"

Then Athena yelled, "HEY, LOSER—want to just do your Blurt now and get it over with? I'll record it for you!"

I yelled back, "I have two weeks, Athena!"

Then she yelled, "I know—it's going to be SOOOO much fun watching you fail!" Then they all laughed their evil little heads off.

I was trying very hard not to cry as I opened my locker. And when I did, I found a note tucked inside by a mysterious stranger.

NOTE FROM
MYSTERIOUS
STRANGER

WANT TO BEAT ATHENA??

I can help...
Meet me at Wagner Cove in Central Park at 3:30 today.

COME ALONE AND TELL NO ONE!!!

My identity must remain a secret

- El Chupacabra

"El Chupacabra"??

CHAPTER 9
THE MYSTERIOUS
CHUPACABRA

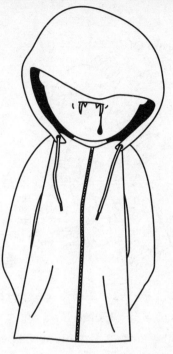

CLAUDIA

My first feeling when I saw the letter was "hopeful."

My second feeling was "suspicious." Because I thought it might just be the Fembots messing with my head.

But then Carmen told me "El Chupacabra" was some kind of mythical vampire-type creature in Mexico who sucks the blood out of goats. And even though I could totally imagine the Fembots as vampires feasting on Mexican farm animals, it didn't seem like a nickname they'd give themselves. Even if they were just trying to mess with my head.

"Chupacabra" = "goat-sucker"

Chupacabra/Fembot

goat

Plus, I was desperate. So I decided to take a chance and meet whoever had written the note. But since the whole thing was very creepy, even though it said to come alone, I took Parvati and Carmen with me.

SOPHIE

I would've had your back, too. But I had ballet after school.

CLAUDIA

No worries, Sophie. I know how hard you've been working on your *grand jeté*.

The note said to meet at Wagner Cove, which is this tucked-away spot in a corner of the Central Park rowboat pond with a little gazebo where teenagers go to make out.

WAGNER COVE: good spot for secret
meetings (and/or teenager makeout sesh)

Before the three of us took the little
path down to the cove, we all got out our
house keys and held them in our fists with the
points sticking out in case we got attacked.

PARVATI

I was totally ready to take down
anybody who messed with us. But when we got
to the gazebo, there was nobody there.

CARMEN

I was thinking, "Maybe it was just a
joke after all."

Then from behind us, this deep, growly,
fake voice went, "I told you to come alone!"

like when
Batman talks
in the movies

CLAUDIA

At first, the voice completely freaked us out.

But then we turned around and realized it was James Mantolini.

Which made total sense. James is easily the strangest person I know. So calling himself "Chupacabra" and making us meet him in secret was probably only about the third-weirdest thing he'd done that day.

James also gets in more trouble than anybody else in the sixth grade. In fact, the whole reason we had to meet in secret was because he was in trouble with the law.

And by "law," I mean "Vice Principal Bevan."

JAMES MANTOLINI, professional troublemaker

I'm technically banned from using the Internet until the end of the school year. If I get caught going online for anything but schoolwork, I'll get expelled.

So if I was going to help you, it had to be on the serious down low.

CLAUDIA

How did you get banned from the Internet?

JAMES

Part of the agreement between my parents and the school is that I can't discuss it. But let's just say Vice Principal Bevan's MUCH more aware of the importance of strong password protection than she used to be. Especially on her online dating profile.

PARVATI

Vice Principal Bevan has an online dating profile?

JAMES

No comment. I've said too much already.

CLAUDIA

Considering the risk he was running, I didn't really understand at first why James was willing to help me.

JAMES

Two reasons: I don't like Fembots, and there was money involved.

CLAUDIA

James said if I won the bet, he wanted half of Athena's $1,000. I was totally fine

with that. But at first, I was a little
doubtful he had the skills to get me to
20,000 Blurt followers.

↖——— Reese had gotten
8,000 MORE FOLLOWERS
just since breakfast

JAMES

    Then I told you about my "Inappropriate
Cockroach" meme.

⊗⊖⊕   **DICTIONARY**

🔍 meme   ✕

meme | mēm | noun
an image, video, etc., that spreads rapidly, usually via
the Internet

CLAUDIA

    I'd never heard of "Inappropriate
Cockroach." But when I googled it, I got a
million hits.

JAMES

    I created that meme. You know how many
hits "Inappropriate Cockroach" got before I
started it? Six.

JAMES'S "INAPPROPRIATE COCKROACH" MEME
(I found dozens of these online)

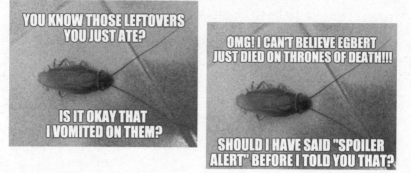

CARMEN

I call nonsense. There's no way you created that meme, James.

PARVATI

I don't believe it, either.

JAMES

It's not necessary for you to believe me. In my heart, I know the truth.

CLAUDIA

I was too desperate to care if James was lying. So I told him he was hired. Then I asked him what the next step was.

JAMES

I said, "First of all, forget trying to make your music videos happen. Only

three kinds of content go viral on Blurt:
stupidity, violence, and cute boys."

CLAUDIA

I said, "Well, I'm definitely not a cute
boy. And I'm not into violence. But I guess
I could try to do something stupid——"

JAMES

I said, "No, no, no. We're not taking
any chances here. You gotta do all three. At
the same time."

Because if you could come up with
Blurts that were stupid, violent, AND had a
cute boy in them? You'd CRUSH it.

CLAUDIA

Doing all three at once seemed
impossible. But James told me to take it one
step at a time. The first thing I needed was
a cute boy who'd be willing to star in my
Blurts.

PARVATI

I suggested Reese. Because tbh? He's
pretty cute.

CLAUDIA

That just seemed wrong. And also kind of
eeew. Plus, the rules of the bet were that
Reese couldn't help me. So if he showed up in
my Blurts, Athena'd say I cheated.

CARMEN

Then I suggested Jens. Because he's not
only totally cute, but he owed you big time for
breaking your heart. AND he felt bad about it,
so you could probably talk him into helping you.

CLAUDIA

This was true. Ever since our breakup,
Jens had been trying to get us to be friends
again. But even though I was mostly over him,
I still thought we should take a break from
talking to each other for a while. Like maybe
ten years. Or more.

When James found out Jens and I broke up,
he said, "Are you really mad at him?"

I said, "Kind of."

JAMES

So I said, "Are you mad enough to hit him
over the head with a baseball bat?"

CLAUDIA

And I said, "A REAL baseball bat? No. I am a peaceful person."

JAMES

Then I said, "What if it was a fake one? Like a Wiffle bat?"

CLAUDIA

I said, "I guess that'd be fine."

JAMES

So that took care of the violence and the cute boy. Then we just needed some stupid to put it over the top.

CLAUDIA

We went through a ton of bad ideas for "stupid" before I remembered the Flubby costume. Ashley's boyfriend, Andy, majored in Musical Theater just like Ashley. So professionally speaking, he's mostly a waiter. But lately, he's also been working as a Times Square cartoon character.

I knew this because a while back, Ashley had showed me a picture of him

OTHER BAD IDEAS:
—clown shoes
—funny hat
—bad singing
—monkey noises
—etc.

hanging out in their apartment wearing a
Flubby costume.

ASHLEY'S BOYFRIEND ANDY (in Flubby costume)
(not sure why he's wearing it while playing Xbox)

For those of you who never had a
childhood and/or weren't allowed to watch TV
when you were little, Flubby's a character
on the TV show *Aardvark Avenue*. Whenever you
go to Times Square, there are at least half
a dozen people standing around in Flubby
costumes, taking pictures with tourists for
money.

I figured I could fit into Andy's
costume because he's pretty short. no offense, Andy!
And he's super nice, so I was 99% sure
he'd let me borrow it.

JAMES

This might sound a little out there...
but when I heard the words "Flubby costume,"
"baseball bat," and "cute boy," EVERYTHING
clicked into place. I had this amazing
vision for a horror story about a Flubby
with a baseball bat chasing a kid through
Central Park.

And I realized the whole reason I'd
been put on this earth was to turn that
vision into a series of the most cunningly
successful Blurts of all time.

PARVATI

It was a little weird when James got
that crazed look in his eye and grabbed you
by the shoulders and went, "Claudia, I AM
GOING TO MAKE YOU A STAR!"

And then he was all, "Actually, no.
You'll be in the Flubby costume. But THE
FLUBBY IS GOING TO BE A STAR!"

Which, BTW, made no sense. Flubby's
ALREADY a star. At least with preschoolers.

CLAUDIA

James almost never makes sense. But I
liked his enthusiasm.

And the more I thought about it, the more it seemed like me putting on a Flubby costume and hitting Jens over the head with a bat could not only go viral and solve my Fembot problem, but might also be very helpful for my healing process.

All I had to do was convince Jens that letting a cartoon character beat him over the head in front of (hopefully) ^millions of people was a good idea.

 +

 +

 = VICTORY!!!
(also HEALING)

CHAPTER 10
REESE AND XANDER^(TRY TO)
TURN PRO

CLAUDIA

Even though everybody at school was drooling all over him, and he'd hit 15,000,000 Blips and 20,000 followers by the time school ended that day, Reese stayed totally down-to-earth and chill. He knew he'd just gotten incredibly lucky, and his moment of being Internet famous was going to end as fast as it started.

So there was NO WAY my brother was going to let it all go to his head, get totally obsessed with becoming a Blurt star, let Xander talk him into a bunch of ridiculous moneymaking ideas, completely embarrass himself trying to make them happen, and just generally lose his mind.

I'm kidding. That's EXACTLY what Reese did.

REESE

That whole day at school, I kept asking to go to the bathroom and then sneaking into a stall to check Blurt on my phone. 'Cause it

was SO AMAZING watching my Blip counter!
It just kept going, "WHHHHZZZZZZZHHHHH!" made-up sound
that means
    I seriously couldn't stop staring at "increasing
it. Once, I lost track of the time when   very fast"
I was in the bathroom, and Mrs. Berner had
to send Dimitri to check on me.

15,444,602 BLIPS

DIMITRI

    I could see Reese's feet under the stall.
So I knocked on the door and said, "Are you
okay?"

    And he went, "I'm blowing up, dude!"

    And I was like, "Yeeeeech. That's really
gross."

    But he didn't mean it like I thought he did.

REESE

    After school, I went over to Xander's
place so we could figure out how to take the
Blurt thing to the next level.

XANDER

    I was all, "Time to turn dem
followers into MAD money!"

21,110
FOLLOWERS

CLAUDIA

    Xander, you DO realize those 20,000

followers were ALL Reese's, right? You had
more like two at that point. Or maybe three,
if your mom had started following you.

XANDER

You just ignorant, Clownia! Me and R-Dog
wuz SHARIN' followers! Cuz we wuz a team!

Xander's nickname for Reese

Plus I wuz doin' all the work. R-Dog
just kept starin' at his Blip counter. I
had to be the one googlin' "how to make dat
Blurt money" and whatnot. *online article Xander googled*

HOW TO MAKE MONEY ON BLURT

It's the hottest social networking site around, and its biggest stars
are turning their millions of followers into millions of dollars. Can
YOU strike it rich on Blurt, too? Read on and find out!

And da article I found told it
straight! All we needed was to hit da trey:
APPEARANCES, BRANDS, and MERCH!

REESE

Appearances are, like, you show up
someplace. And people give you money just
for being there. Like at that BlurtUp thing.

XANDER

So I emailed dem BlurtUp bruhs. And I was all, "Yo, Skronkmonsters be ready to get with you! Hook us up on dat main stage, y'all!"

XANDER (email to BlurtUp.com)

X ← ⇐ → ✉

From: XIzKillinIt@gmail.com
To: Marketing@BlurtUp.com
Date: 03/13/17 4:35:06 PM EST
Subject: SKRONKMONSTERS AVAIL 4 BLURTUP NYC!!!!!

WUT UP BLURTUP PEEPS!

SKRONKMONSTER AND SKRONKMONSTER_X CAN B AT BLURTUP NYC NEXT WEEK.

WE R GETTIN HUGE (20K NOW, PROB 1M+ BY NEXT WEEK) SO YOU SHOULD JUMP ONIT

HIT US BACK AND SAY HOW MUCH U WLL PAY

WE R LOCAL SO WE DONT NEED HOTEL. JUST LIMOS N WHATNOT

SKRONKMONSTER_X

CLAUDIA

(sarcasm) → I would like to pause here to say I was completely shocked when I found out nobody at BlurtUp ever emailed Xander back.

XANDER

They best hope it went to junk mail. 'Cause don't nobody disrespect the X-Man.

REESE

Then Xander was like, "Step Two: BRANDS!"

XANDER

Brands is endorsements! Skronkmonster sellin' product to da people!

REESE

So brand deals are, like, you post a Blurt going, "I LOVE RUSH SODA! EVERYBODY SHOULD DRINK IT!"

And then Rush Soda pays you a bunch of money for hyping their stuff.

CLAUDIA

Right...Except for that to actually work, you have to get Rush Soda to agree to pay you BEFORE you post the Blurt.

REESE

Yeah...but the article Xander read didn't say that. So we just did the Blurt first.

But, like, there aren't any soda cans or bottles or whatever in MetaWorld? So we used a log. 'Cause they're kinda soda-can-shaped.

But it was tough to, like, draw a Rush Soda logo on the log, so we drew it on a wall, too. Then we had my avatar stand by the wall and hold up the log like he was drinking it.

I wasn't totally sure it looked good. But Xander was all, "BLURT IT SO WE CAN CASH IN!"

So I did. Then Xander went on the Rush Soda website and told them to give us some money.

SKRONK DRINKZ RUSH!

XANDER

Rush Soda didn't have no email. Just a form that wuz all, "We value your feedback."

So I filled it out like, "You BEST value this feedback! Skronkmonster be REPRESENTIN' for yo' brand! Peep this Blurt link, yo! Then hit us back with dat mad cheeeez!"

They still ain't hit us back yet. *in Xander-speak, this means "give us money"*

CLAUDIA

(more sarcasm)

Once again, I am shocked that Rush Soda never "hit them back" and/or sent Xander and Reese a bunch of money in exchange for a Blurt of Reese's avatar pretending to drink a log.

REESE

Then Xander was like, "Step Three: Merch!"

Which is short for "Merchandise." So it's, like, selling people "Skronkmonster" T-shirts and phone cases and stuff.

And I was psyched for that. Like, I was thinking how awesome it'd be if I walked down the street and saw somebody wearing a "Skronkmonster" T-shirt. I'd be like, "That's ME! High five!"

But then Xander googled "how to get rich selling T-shirts online." And it turns out it's mad hard.

XANDER

Dem article wuz all, "Five Things You Need to Know About Sellin' T's!" And number one wuz "You Ain't Gonna Make No Money On It!"

So I didn't even read dem other four.

1. SELLING T-SHIRTS ONLINE (PROBABLY) WON'T MAKE YOU RICH

The good news is that setting up your online T-shirt business couldn't be simpler! The bad news is that with low margins and thousands of competitors, 99% of sellers will never earn more than a modest amount of money.

REESE

When I went home for dinner, I was thinking even without T-shirts, we were in great shape.

Because I figured BlurtUp would pay us to show up there.

no, they wouldn't

And Rush Soda was going to pay us for the Blurt we'd just posted. no, they weren't

And that new Blurt was going to blow up just like the first one did! no, it wasn't

So I was SUPER excited for what was going to happen next.

he shouldn't have been (srsly)

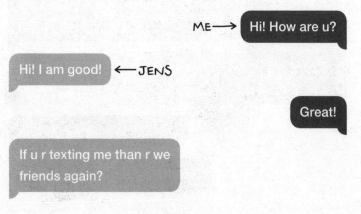

CHAPTER 11
ATTACK OF THE
FOLLOWERS

CLAUDIA

After I got home that afternoon and made sure Ashley's boyfriend was cool with loaning me his Flubby costume, I texted Jens.

It was our first official communication since the breakup.

CLAUDIA AND JENS (text messages)

ME→ Hi! How are u?

Hi! I am good! ←JENS

Great!

If u r texting me than r we friends again?

Possibly. I am wondering if you will do me a big favor

Yes sure anything

Are you busy this weekend?

I have soccer game Sunday. But Saturday free

Would you be ok with me hitting you over the head with a fake baseball bat in Central Park while I wear a Flubby costume and Carmen records it for a Blurt?

I think my English is not good enough to understand this

Your English is fine. It's just a very strange favor

You want me to play baseball in park with Carmen and Fluuber?

OK maybe it's your English

FaceTiming you now to explain

CLAUDIA

It took a while to get Jens to understand what I wanted him to do. Then it took even longer to get him to agree to it. By the time he did, the rest of my family was home. And because it was Friday night, we all went out for dinner.

HAN DYNASTY: v. good Chinese (also v. spicy)

Dad had just gotten a Blurt account that day so he could understand what was going on with me and Reese. Or at least try to. Because Dad was having a very hard time figuring out Blurt.

DAD AND MOM (text messages)

I got a Blurt account!

I'll follow you. What's your username?

I don't have one

That is literally impossible

You definitely have one

I am MomSeesAllSoBehave

Follow me and I will follow back

How do I follow you?

Click search button and type in my username

Can't find search button

Bottom left on home screen

Can't find home screen

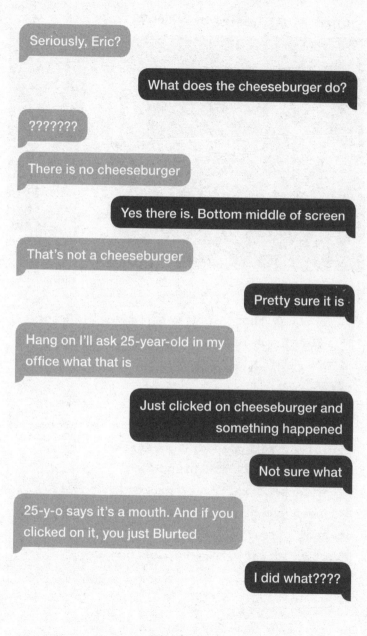

Seriously, Eric?

What does the cheeseburger do?

???????

There is no cheeseburger

Yes there is. Bottom middle of screen

That's not a cheeseburger

Pretty sure it is

Hang on I'll ask 25-year-old in my office what that is

Just clicked on cheeseburger and something happened

Not sure what

25-y-o says it's a mouth. And if you clicked on it, you just Blurted

I did what????

DAD'S FIRST BLURT (posted by accident)

Eric.S.Tapper

23 BLIPS

CLAUDIA

Dinner that night was a real disaster. I'll let Reese explain why.

REESE

Mom and Dad have this rule that we can't use our phones at the dinner table. But after we ordered, I was like, "Who wants to see my new Blurt?"

'Cause I was crazy excited about it. I'd been checking the Blip counter, and it hadn't really taken off yet. But I figured it was going to blow up any minute.

TABLE MANNERS

CLAUDIA

Serious question: why did you think a Blurt of your avatar pretending to drink a log was going to be popular? I mean, why would anybody want to watch that?

REESE

Huh...I guess when you put it that way, it DOES seem pretty stupid.

I think I just figured the last one got huge, so this one would, too?

Or something?

Anyway, I asked Mom and Dad if I could take out my phone to show them the Blurt.

And they were like, "No phones at dinner!" But I just kept bugging them. I was like, "It's only two seconds long! C'mon! I worked really hard on it!"

Finally, Mom was like, "Fine. But we're watching it on MY phone." So she got her phone out, and she and Dad watched my Blurt.

CLAUDIA

At first, Mom and Dad just looked confused. Mom said something like, "I'm not sure I get this...."

And Dad said, "Why is he hitting himself in the face with a block of wood?"

REESE

I started explaining it to them. But then I guess Mom must've scrolled down to look at the comments. Because all of a sudden she was like, "REEEESE! THE LANGUAGE!!!"

CLAUDIA

Mom and Dad's other big rule besides "no cell phones at dinner" is "no swearing on social media." Not only do they not let me and Reese use bad language online, but if anybody else swears when they comment on one of our posts, Mom and Dad make us delete THAT person's comment, too.

This is because they believe everything that happens on your online accounts is a reflection of you as a person. So if you let people swear on your ClickChat page, or your Blurt page, or wherever, when you grow up and want to get a job, employers will google you and see the swearing and decide not to hire you.

This actually makes a ton of sense to me.

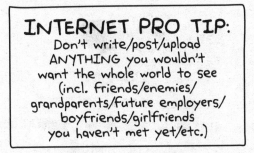

INTERNET PRO TIP:
Don't write/post/upload
ANYTHING you wouldn't
want the whole world to see
(incl. friends/enemies/
grandparents/future employers/
boyfriends/girlfriends
you haven't met yet/etc.)

REESE

Reese's career
goals = not
realistic

Not me. I'm either going to be a professional soccer player or a Blurt star when I grow up. Either way, I don't think swearing on my Blurt page is going to be a deal breaker.

CLAUDIA

It turned out Reese's new Blurt was NOT going over well with his 22,000 followers. And they were letting him know it. So when Mom looked at the comment section, it was basically Curse-O-Rama.

BLURT COMMENT SECTION

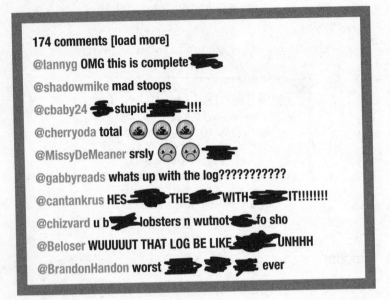

174 comments [load more]

@lannyg **OMG this is complete**▓▓

@shadowmike **mad stoops**

@cbaby24 ▓▓**stupid**▓▓▓**!!!**

@cherryoda **total** 💩💩💩

@MissyDeMeaner **srsly** 😞😞▓▓

@gabbyreads **whats up with the log???????????**

@cantankrus **HES**▓▓**THE**▓▓**WITH**▓▓**IT!!!!!!!!**

@chizvard **u b**▓▓**lobsters n wutnot**▓▓**fo sho**

@Beloser **WUUUUUT THAT LOG BE LIKE**▓▓**UNHHH**

@BrandonHandon **worst**▓▓▓▓ **ever**

REESE

Mom lost it. She was like, "Delete these comments or I'm shutting down your account!"

I was like, "What comments?" 'Cause all I'd been looking at was the Blip counter. I'd forgotten Blurts even HAD comments.

So I took out my phone. But then Mom was like, "No phones at the table!"

Which seriously did not make sense. How was I going to delete the comments if I couldn't use my phone?

CLAUDIA

Mom takes the "no phones at the table" rule very seriously. But she ALSO takes the "no swearing on social media" rule very seriously. So the situation pretty much made her head explode.

She told Reese he had thirty seconds to delete all the comments with swearing in them. But when he saw the comments, Reese suddenly realized his new Blurt was a disaster. And his career as a Blurt star might be over before it started.

So he COMPLETELY freaked out.

REESE

I didn't know what to do! I was like, "I gotta delete this whole Blurt! But I can't! 'Cause what if Rush Soda wants to pay me for it? But everybody's hating on it! And what if I lose all my followers? I should tell them I'm sorry! But they're saying really mean stuff! So I should defend myself! Or maybe I should just block all of them? I gotta talk to Xander! AND WHY WON'T MOM STOP YELLING AT ME???!!!"

CLAUDIA

Basically, dinner that night was dumplings, kung pao chicken, yelling, and tears.

It was so bad that six weeks later, Mom's still too embarrassed to go back to Han Dynasty. Mom read this and said, "Give it another month"

After we got home that night and he talked to Xander, Reese wound up deleting the whole soda/log Blurt. And if he'd been smart, he would've realized he was in way over his head, and he should just be happy with his one insanely successful Blurt and quit trying to make a whole career out of it.

Unfortunately, he wasn't smart.

CHAPTER 12
JAMES MANTOLINI,
VISIONARY BLURT ARTIST

FILM
THE FURRY MENACE
DIRECTOR
JAMES MANTOLINI
TAKE #1,007

CLAUDIA

Reese spent the whole weekend in full panic mode about his Blurt career. But I wasn't paying attention to him, because I was too busy sweating my brains out inside a Flubby costume while James Mantolini screamed at me in Central Park.

For five hours. Which was four hours and fifty-five minutes longer than Jens and I had expected the shoot to last.

It was very unpleasant.

James (yelling) →

me (getting yelled at)

Jens (also getting yelled at)

(photo credit: Carmen)

JENS KUYPERS, Dutch soccer player/ heartbreaker/amateur Blurt actor

The whole time, I am thinking, "Why does this take so long? A Blurt is two seconds!"

Nobody told to me that we are making thirty-seven of them.

Also, I did not like James screaming at me so much.

JAMES, professional crazy person/Blurt video director

You can't make an omelet without breaking some eggs.

And I wasn't fooling around. I had
personally set out to create the most
captivating, viral-ready Blurts of all
time. My goal wasn't just to pile up 30,000
followers on Claudia's account—I wanted to
create an episodic, short-form cinematic
experience SO AMAZING it'd revolutionize the
entire medium and change people's ideas of
what a Blurt could be forever.

So I don't think you should be asking
yourselves, "Did James scream at me?"

I think you should be asking, "Did
James achieve his creative vision for the
project, while getting the absolutely best
performance possible out of me?"

And I think the Blurts speak for
themselves.

CLAUDIA

The Blurts actually did turn out
amazing. James created a whole story about
a cute boy getting stalked by a deranged
Flubby in Central Park, then broke it up
into dozens of two-second Blurts. And some
of them were HILARIOUS.

They were also weird and creepy. But in
a good way.

still frame from <u>THE FURRY MENACE</u>
(Blurt #12) (out of 37)

JAMES

The official title of the piece was *The Furry Menace*. Stylistically, it was heavily influenced by the work of Italian director Dario Argento. Also, Road Runner cartoons.

"disgruntled" = angry/annoyed

CARMEN, disgruntled director

James is just completely full of himself. It's like he thinks he's Steven Spielberg.

JAMES

That's ridiculous. I was aiming MUCH higher than Steven Spielberg. He just has to make one movie at a time. I made THIRTY-SEVEN Blurts—each one totally self-contained, but also telling one thirty-seventh of a larger story.

CLAUDIA

Carmen is very bitter about the whole situation. Because she thought SHE was going to be directing the Blurts, just like she directed my music video.

But when she showed up, James told her she could only direct "second unit."

CARMEN

I still don't know what that means. All I know is James is a monster. And two hours of him screaming was all I could handle. So I left early.

JAMES

It's actually a real shame Carmen left early. We needed her to help keep the tourists out of the shots.

tourist who ruined shot

CLAUDIA

The tourists were a real problem. And not just because they kept wandering into the background of the shots.

It turns out that if you wear a Flubby costume anywhere in New York City, tourists will assume you're there to take pictures with them.

And a lot of tourists don't speak English. So when they'd come up to me and want to take a picture, it was VERY hard to explain to them that I wasn't that kind of Flubby.

Eventually, I realized it was easier to just let them take the pictures.

me
(Flubby)

non–English–
speaking tourist
(paid me 5 bucks
for pic)

The good news was that they paid me for
them. So I made thirty dollars. I gave all
of it to Jens, because I felt very guilty
about getting him involved. And not just
because the shoot took five hours, and James
was screaming at him the whole time.

I also felt guilty because we found out
even a fake baseball bat really hurts when
someone beats you over the head with it.

THE FURRY MENACE
(#33 of 37)
(in video, Jens's
screaming was
100% real)
(b/c I got a
little carried away)

JENS

I am thinking, "Okay, bat is just made from plastic. How much can it hurt?"

But the answer is, "A lot." My head has pain for total three days after that.

JAMES

Hey, man—if you want to make great art, sometimes you have to suffer for it.

THE FURRY MENACE (#37 of 37)
(FINAL SHOT)

CHAPTER 13
REESE JUMPS
THE SHARK

CLAUDIA

While I was getting yelled at wearing a Flubby costume in Central Park, Reese and Xander were taking their Blurt career to the next level.

Unfortunately for them, the next level was lower than their last level.

REESE

After we deleted the Rush Soda Blurt, Xander and I knew we had to post more content. My first Blurt was still getting Blips, but it was definitely slowing down a ton. And my followers were stuck around 25,000.

So we needed a totally awesome follow-up. I wanted to do something at LEAST twice as funny as jumping off a tower.

XANDER

So I was all, "Just make the tower twice as tall, yo!"

REESE

That seemed like a good idea. (not a good idea) So we spent all Saturday morning building this REEAAAAALLLY tall tower on MetaWorld.

But it was so tall that when Xander's avatar jumped off, it took four seconds to hit the ground. And Blurts are only two seconds long. So we couldn't use it.

REESE'S VERY TALL TOWER (actually TOO tall)

71406 MK/21965003 GZ
01:54:16

Then I thought, "What if I run into
something really fast? Like a wall?" So then
it'd be like the "SPLAAAT!" when we fell off
the tower, except sideways.

So we tried running our avatars into
walls. But it turns out you can't run fast
enough to splat against a wall. You just
kinda hit the wall and go, "NNNGGGHHH."

Then I thought, "What if I shoot myself
out of a cannon?"

XANDER

Dat cannon idea was siiiiiiiick!
'Cept we needed a cannon.

REESE

It's not like there's cannons just lying
around in MetaWorld. If you want one, you
pretty much have to mod it yourself. So you
need to know how to code.　　mod = modify = create a
custom object in MetaWorld
Which Xander and I were clueless about.
So I asked Akash, 'cause he's, like, a genius
at computer stuff.

AKASH

So it's Saturday afternoon, and I'm
sitting at home binge-watching *Captain*

Impossible episodes when your brother messages me on ClickChat.

CLICKCHAT POSTS (PRIVATE CHAT)

Reese (Skronkmonster) Hey Akash wt up r u there?

Akash (AmigoGod) y

Skronkmonster Can u build me a cannon????

AmigoGod I'm assuming you mean a MetaWorld cannon and not a real one? Or is there some kind of civil war going on in your apartment building?

Skronkmonster yah sorry MW canon

Skronkmonster not real one

Skronkmonster want to shoot myelf out of it for a Blurt

AmigoGod Sure. Fifty bucks

Skronkmonster R u serius???????

Skronkmonster Thats cray

AmigoGod You're right. Fifty's way too low. Make it a hundred

[Skronkmonster has invited Skronkmonster_X to the chat]

Xander (Skronkmonster_X) YO AK-47 WUT DISH ISH BOUT U OVERCHARGN??? ← Xander's nickname for Akash

AmigoGod Hello, Mrs. Skronkmonster! How's married life?

Skronkmonster_X NOT FUNNY YO

Skronkmonster_X WE NEED A CANON STAT

AmigoGod If Xander's involved, it'll be two hundred

Skronkmonster_X DON'T MAKE ME SMACK DA TASTE OUTTA YO MOUF

AmigoGod Three hundred

> Skronkmonster **can u log off X?**
>
> Skronkmonster_X **THESE COLORS DONT RUN**
>
> *[Skronkmonster has blocked Skronkmonster_X from the chat]*
>
> AmigoGod **Smart move**
>
> Skronkmonster **Can u pleeeeeeeeeez build it? I dont have money but its super impartnt**
>
> AmigoGod **I'll do it for 20% of your revenues and a chocolate cigar from Hot & Crusty**   *Akash's favorite snack food*
>
> Skronkmonster **Are revenus money**
>
> AmigoGod **Yes, but there won't be any. Because you're clueless. But bring me a chocolate cigar in the next 90 minutes and I'll build you a cannon**

REESE

So Akash built us this awesome cannon.

AKASH

I didn't actually build it. I downloaded it from a freeware site. It took thirty seconds. But I got those idiots to deliver a chocolate cigar to my door for free! Which really improved my *Captain Impossible* marathon.

REESE

Making a Blurt with the cannon wasn't as easy as we thought. 'Cause number one, it takes a LOT longer than two seconds to load yourself into a cannon and fire it.

And number two, when you shoot yourself out of a cannon, it doesn't, like, launch you into the air. It just blows your whole body to bits.

But not in a funny way. A sad way.

Then Xander had a total brainstorm.

XANDER

Xander "brainstorm" =
"cloudy with occasional drizzle"

I wuz all, "Just stand there and blow your head off!"

REESE

So I put my head in front of the cannon barrel and blew it off. And THAT was hilarious!

So we Blurted it. And we were like, "This is going to be huge!"

REESE/XANDER'S CANNON BLURT...

skronkmonster   23,485 BLIPS

71406 MK/21965894 GZ
00:21:16

AWWWW NOO!!! MY HEDZ BLOWN OFF!!!
#MetaWorld

And it turned out it WAS huge...when
BewBewBoy posted the exact same Blurt two
years ago.

...AND BEWBEWBOY'S CANNON BLURT
(2+ years old) (3rd most popular Blurt in history)

BewBewBoy   1,764,847,382 BLIPS

1453846 MK / 313848591 GZ
00:02:55

ouch

And then I guess a gazillion other
people copied it.

So by the time we did it, blowing your
head off with a cannon on Blurt wasn't cool
anymore. It was just lame. And we got flamed
pretty bad in the comments.

XANDER

Dem comments was COLD, yo!

BLURT COMMENT SECTION

used to be 100+ comments, but Reese
had to delete the ones w/swearing

5 comments

@gabbyreads **omg so lame**

@shadowmike **BewBewBoy shuld sue them**

@MissyDeMeaner 💩 💩 💩 💩

@everythingIlike **it was funny the first 700000000 times I saw it**

@cantankrus **UNFOLLOW**

REESE

The worst part wasn't even the haters in the comments. It was that after we posted it, I lost 1,000 followers. And I freaked. I was like, "People are leaving! We gotta post something else STAT!"

23,861 FOLLOWERS (was over 25,000 before cannon Blurt)

But all we had was the super-tall tower thing. Which was four seconds. So we split it into two Blurts and posted both of them.

And then we lost 3,000 more followers. 'Cause everybody hated them. People in the comments were all, "They jumped the shark!"

> @DannysInVegas **wow @Skronkmonster done jumped the shark**
>
> @clevercooky **aaaaand we've jumped the shark**
>
> @Wereworlder **sad shark is sad. "Y U JUMP ME?"**

I didn't even know what "jump the shark" meant. So I had to look it up. And it was NOT good.

❌➖➕   **DICTIONARY**

🔍 jump the shark| ✕

jump the shark | slang
the point when a TV or film series exhausts its creative potential and begins a rapid decline in quality marked by the inclusion of desperate and/or implausible events (refers to an episode of the *Happy Days* TV series in which the "Fonzie" character jumped over a shark while on water skis)

CLAUDIA

If you think about it, this was actually impressive. Most TV shows don't jump the shark until after a hundred episodes. Reese and Xander did it after just one Blurt.

CHAPTER 14
THE FURRY MENACE SAVES MY LIFE

CLAUDIA

By the time we went back to school on
Monday, Reese had fallen from his Saturday-
morning peak of 25,000 followers all the way
down to 21,000.

Reese → 21,088 FOLLOWERS   217 FOLLOWERS ← me

Which was encouraging...but still 20,800
followers more than I had. So I was pretty
desperate to start posting the *Furry Menace*
Blurts. I'd been bugging James to let me get
started ever since we'd finished shooting in
Central Park on Saturday.

CLAUDIA AND JAMES (text messages)

Hi! Are the Blurts done yet?

Most of them. Doing some post-production

Can you send me the first ones so I can post?

Will put them on thumb drive and bring to school tomorrow

Can't you just email them?

What part of "I'm banned from the Internet" don't you understand?

Oh, right. Sorry!

While you're waiting, you should join other social networks

Then you can cross-post to drive more traffic

Great idea. Which sites should I join?

Right now I am only on ClickChat and Blurt

Join Flippy, Blather, Bloop, GrabBag, Readr, Shout, and Kimchi

Are all those real?

Yes

I just checked out Kimchi and, ummm...it's in Korean

Sign up anyway. Use Google translate

Srsly?

Trust me. Furry Menace will go over HUGE in Korea

CLAUDIA

I joined all the sites James told me to join, including Kimchi.

At least, I THINK I joined Kimchi. When I put the confirmation email I got through Google Translate, it said, "Congratulations!

You can use the brine close. If you can be used to set, press here."

So I'm not totally sure what my status is over there.

Then I linked all the sites to Blurt so they'd cross-post whenever I Blurted. But since I didn't get the thumb drive with all the Blurts from James until Monday morning, I had to wait until after school that day to start posting.

THE THUMB DRIVE JAMES GAVE ME

SPOILER ALERT:
pointy ears will be
v. important
later in story

There were eleven days left in the bet, so James put me on a four-Blurt-a-day schedule. He also told me when to post, what hashtags to use, which Blurt stars to tag in the comments, and how to lie to people so nobody would know he had anything to do with it.

official story:
my weird cousin
asked me and
Jens to help with
his student film

JAMES

Speaking as an artist, not being able to take credit for my work was very painful.

But not as painful as getting expelled would've been if Vice Principal Bevan caught me going online.

And I figured I could always reveal my identity after the school year ended and *The Furry Menace* had become a massive global phenomenon.

CLAUDIA

I posted the first four Blurts every two hours between 3:30 and 9:30pm on Monday. And for a massive global phenomenon, they got off to a very slow start.

THE FURRY MENACE
(Blurt #1 of 37)

claudaroo   864 BLIPS

THE FURRY MENACE #1

In fact, it was such a slow start that on Tuesday morning, I had to hide out in the library again before school to avoid getting laughed at by the Fembots.

And when I passed them in the hallway before second period and Athena yelled, "Nice try, Claudia! Lamest Blurts EVER!" I got a horrible sick feeling in my stomach because I thought she might be right.

I was so worried that—since some of the Blurts were much funnier than others—I asked James if we should rethink the strategy and release the funniest ones first.

JAMES

That was ridiculous. Would you ask Herman Melville to shuffle chapters of *Moby-Dick* around to get to the whale faster?

CLAUDIA

I don't know. I've never read *Moby-Dick*.

JAMES

You wouldn't like it. There's no cute boys.

CLAUDIA

That is very sexist, James.

Anyway, by the end of school on Tuesday, the first four Blurts were picking up steam. They each had over 8,000 Blips, and I'd gotten seventy-five new followers.

292
FOLLOWERS

And when I released Blurts #5–8 that night, *The Furry Menace* really started to get some traction.

PARVATI

Can I just say, number 6 was my personal favorite? It was like a scene from an actual movie.

claudaroo   64,321 BLIPS

THE FURRY MENACE #6

WYATT

Those first four Blurts were just
weird. I didn't really understand what was
going on at all. I was like, "Reese, did
your sister have a mental breakdown or
something?"

But then when the next four came out
and the Flubby started chasing Jens, I
was like, "Wait a minute—this is actually
INSANELY COOL."

JENS

At the first, I didn't watch them.
Because I did not have the Blurt account.

And also my head was still hurting
from the bat. So I just wanted to forget
whole thing.

But then after soccer practice Tuesday,
there was new Blurts, and Wyatt shows
everybody them on his phone. And the whole
team is saying, "This is great!"

So I make a Blurt account to watch.
And almost right away I get fifty followers!

CLAUDIA

By Wednesday after school, six of the

eight Blurts had over 40,000 Blips, #6 had
60,000 Blips, and I was closing
in on 1,000 followers.

Then I released #9-12, and
things REALLY started to take off.

claudaroo   26,855 BLIPS

THE FURRY MENACE #10

It was so exciting that I basically got
zero homework done that whole night.

CLICKCHAT POSTS (PRIVATE CHAT)

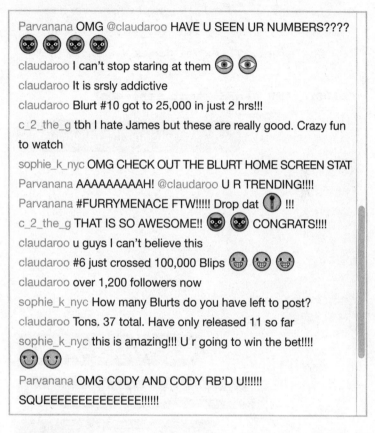

Parvanana OMG @claudaroo HAVE U SEEN UR NUMBERS???? 😼 😼 😼 😼

claudaroo I can't stop staring at them 👁 👁

claudaroo It is srsly addictive

claudaroo Blurt #10 got to 25,000 in just 2 hrs!!!

c_2_the_g tbh I hate James but these are really good. Crazy fun to watch

sophie_k_nyc OMG CHECK OUT THE BLURT HOME SCREEN STAT

Parvanana AAAAAAAAAH! @claudaroo U R TRENDING!!!!

Parvanana #FURRYMENACE FTW!!!!! Drop dat 🎤 !!!

c_2_the_g THAT IS SO AWESOME!! 😼 😼 CONGRATS!!!!

claudaroo u guys I can't believe this

claudaroo #6 just crossed 100,000 Blips 😁 😁 😁

claudaroo over 1,200 followers now

sophie_k_nyc How many Blurts do you have left to post?

claudaroo Tons. 37 total. Have only released 11 so far

sophie_k_nyc this is amazing!!! U r going to win the bet!!!! 😊 😊

Parvanana OMG CODY AND CODY RB'D U!!!!!! SQUEEEEEEEEEEEEEE!!!!!!

CLAUDIA

By the time I went to bed that night, #FurryMenace had been trending on the Blurt home screen for two hours, a couple of Blurt stars had RB'ed it, and I was up to over 1,500 followers.

James's plan was working—I was actually starting to go viral. So right before Mom came in and made me put away my electronics for the night, I texted James to thank him.

CLAUDIA AND JAMES (text messages)

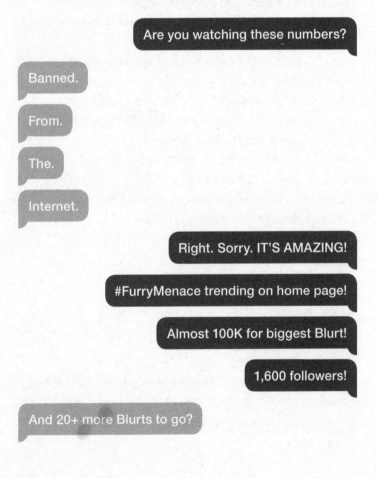

Are you watching these numbers?

Banned.

From.

The.

Internet.

Right. Sorry. IT'S AMAZING!

#FurryMenace trending on home page!

Almost 100K for biggest Blurt!

1,600 followers!

And 20+ more Blurts to go?

Exactly

THANK YOU SO MUCH JAMES!!!!!!
YOU ARE A ROCK STAR

Yes I am

I COULD NOT HAVE DONE THIS
WITHOUT YOU

You really couldn't

Just don't tell anybody I was involved

I won't. I promise

Unless somebody wants to make a
film/TV deal

That'd be worth getting expelled over

OK

Congrats—u r going to be bigger
than that kid who bit his brother's
finger

CLAUDIA

Speaking of brothers...while I was lying
in bed dreaming of victory over the Fembots,
Reese was spiraling down into a waking
nightmare from which there was no escape.

And by "waking nightmare," I mean the
comment section of his Blurt page.

CHAPTER 15
REESE FALLS DOWN THE
COMMENT HOLE

CLAUDIA

While I was gaining followers that week, Reese was losing them. Along with his mind.

REESE

It was all Mom's fault. 'Cause she's the one who kept telling me she was going to shut down my account if she found any bad language on my Blurt page.

But every time I deleted all the comments that had bad language, the trolls who wrote them just commented again with WORSE language!

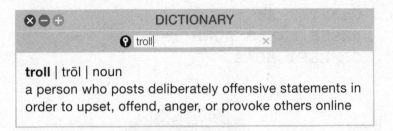

troll | trōl | noun
a person who posts deliberately offensive statements in order to upset, offend, anger, or provoke others online

BLURT COMMENT SECTION

342 comments [load more]
@urkelslovechild ▬▬▬U @skronkmonster ▬ ▬

@cantankrus ▬ ▬ ▬!!!!!!!
@Beloser ▬ ▬ ▬ ▬
@chizvard ▬ ▬
@BrandonHandon Delete me agin and Ill ▬ ▬ ▬
you▬

CLAUDIA

Why didn't you just block all their accounts?

REESE

I did! They kept coming back with different usernames!

BLURT COMMENT SECTION

> **52 comments [load more]**
>
> @Bewinner **AWWWWW WIDDLE BABY BLOCK DA BAD MEN BWWAAAA**
>
> @Brandon_Handon **block this @skronkmonster u** ▬▬▬
> ▬▬
>
> @revengeofurkel **U CANT HANDUL THE TRUTH**
>
> @01chizvard **hey @skronkmonster ur village called its missing an idiot**
>
> @cantankrus25 **u r such a** ▬▬▬

REESE

It was seriously stressing me out. Like, I'd delete fifty comments, and an hour later, there'd be fifty more! It was totally cray.

So I asked Xander what we should do to get rid of the trolls. And he was like, "I'ma lay some smack down!"

And that just made it ten times worse. Especially when the trolls all started calling themselves "Skronkmonster."

BLURT COMMENT SECTION

107 comments [load more]

Xander →@Skronkmonster_X **BEST RUN @01chizvard U IN MY HOUSE NOW**

@Skronkmonster_X **SAME 2 U @Brandon_Handon U A STRAIGHT PUNK**

trolls imitating Xander →@Skronkmonster_Z **im a widdle baby and I just pooped my pants**

@Skronkmonster_Z **waa waa waah**

@01chizvard **^^^^^ awesome username!!!**

@Skronkmonster_X **NOT COOL YO DELETE THAT SCREENAME NOW**

@Skronkmonster_B **B is for baby!!!!!!**

@Skronkmonster_B **IMA WIDDLE BABY SKWONKMONSTAW**

@cantankrus25 **BWAHAHAHAHAHA**

@Skronkmonster_X **SRSLY U CAN'T DO THAT U R NOT SKRONKMONSTERS**

@Skronkmonster_Y **^^^^ AND THA Y IS FOR YES I CAN!!!!! ^^^^**

@Skronkmonster_D **and the D is for DUUUUUUUUH**

@Skronkmonster_Z **OMG TOO FUNNY**

@Skronkmonster_P **P IS FOR PWNNNNED**

REESE

   I freaked out and blocked all the
usernames from "Skronkmonster_A" to

except X (which was Xander)
"Skronkmonster_Z." But then they started
using numbers. And there was no way to
block all the numbers. 'Cause numbers are
infinite!

   After that, all I could think about
was how to stop the trolls. Wednesday
afternoon, I had such a bad soccer practice
that afterwards, Coach Unger wanted to know
if everything was okay at home.

   I seriously needed help. So I texted Dad
for advice.

REESE AND DAD (text messages)

> Dad trolls keep flaming me in comments and I cant get rid of them what do I do???

> What are trolls?

> And what's flaming?

> NM Ill ask mom

> What's NM?

REESE AND MOM (text messages)

> Mom thes trolls keep flaming me on Blurt how do I make them stop??

Block their accounts

> I did they just got new usernames

Try ignoring them. Maybe they will get bored and go away

> I m ignoring them!!!!

> I NEVER reply

> It doesnt help

> Also will u let me stop deleting swear words? I think its making them mad

NO. KEEP DELETING

REESE

That night, I deleted, like, a hundred comments and blocked everybody who wrote

them. But they just kept commenting more
under different names!

Then at 9:30, Mom came in and made me
put away my electronics for the night.

CLAUDIA

Mom and Dad have a policy that we
can't go to sleep with any electronics ←
in our bedrooms. This is because they —laptops
don't want us staying up all night   —phones
online and/or going on the Internet   —ipads
before we even get out of bed in the —etc.
morning.

REESE

So I put my laptop in the kitchen and
went to bed. But while I was lying there, I
thought, "If ignoring them and deleting them
isn't working...and Xander yelling at them
didn't work...maybe I should just try to talk
to the trolls and ask them to be cool."

INTERNET PRO TIP:
DON'T FEED THE TROLLS!
Mom was right—if there are
trolls in your comment section,
do NOT try to argue with them.
They will only get worse.

So I snuck out to the kitchen and got
my laptop from where Mom left it. I was just
going to write one little message. But then
it turned into a whole thing.

BLURT COMMENT SECTION

134 comments [load more]

@Skronkmonster hey other skronkmonsters can u be chill i
m just trying to make some fun Blurts if u dont like it thats
cool then y not just ignore it? Im not hurting anyone n I dont
want to fight anybody

@Skronkmonster_05 awwwwww is sad skronkmonster sad?

@Skronkmonster_32 poor widdle baby

@Skronkmonster_414 u r the worst @skronkmonster

@Skronkmonster y would u say that????? U don't no me at all

@Skronkmonster_909 ur Blurts r lame

@Skronkmonster ok fine so dont watch them

@Skronkmonster_909 n u copied off BewBewBoy

@Skronkmonster not on purpos we deleted that one

@jenna_in_FL @skronkmonster I THINK U R AWESUM JUST
IGNORE THESE H8RS

@Skronkmonster thx @jenna_in_FL!!!

@Skronkmonster_909 sock puppet

@izzymarbles U R THE BEST @skronkmonster KEEP POSTING

@Skronkmonster thx @izzymarbles!

@Skronkmonster_32 wut happened did preskool just let out

REESE

When other people started sticking
up for me, I was like, "This is awesome!
They're like troll fighters! I have a troll-
fighting army!"

So they started ripping the trolls
with me, and the trolls ripped us back,
and a bunch of people got into it, and then
somebody started talking about politics, and
it got mad confusing, and it just kept going
on and on, and then before I knew it Mom was
at my bedroom door in her pajamas, yelling
"WHAT ARE YOU DOING UP AT THIS HOUR?"

And that's when I realized it was 3:00am.

BLURT COMMENT SECTION

2,113 comments [load more]   OMG this is INSANE
                               number of comments
@jenna_in_FL 1st avengers movie was way better
@Skronkmonster_414 ur just ignorunt
@Skronkmonster g2g

CLAUDIA

After that, Mom and Dad decided Reese
needed a break from Blurt. So they took away
all his electronics for at least a week.

REESE

    I was actually kind of glad they did it.
Being on Blurt was really starting to grumpf
me out. After I got off it, I just
wanted to, like, go outside and sit on
a rock and stare at trees for a while.

not sure what this means ("stress"? "burn"?)

    But when Xander found out, he got
totally skronked.

XANDER

    I's all, "You can't punk out on me,
bruh! I'm fixin' to drop a MAD Blurt! We
gonna blow the roof off this mutha!"

REESE

    Xander had this idea for a new Blurt he
was really hyped about. When I told him I
couldn't go online and post it, he said he'd
do it himself if I just gave him my Blurt
password.

CLAUDIA

    But you didn't give it to him, right?
Because Mom and Dad have been telling us
for YEARS to NEVER give our passwords to
ANYBODY.

REESE

Yeah...Mom and Dad were right. That was really good advice.

I seriously wish I'd taken it.

CHAPTER 16
WHAT COULD POSSIBLY GO WRONG?

CLAUDIA

When I found out at breakfast on Thursday that Mom and Dad had kicked Reese off the Internet for a week, I felt bad for my brother. Not only was his dream of being a Blurt star crumbling into dust, but after staying up all night fighting trolls, he looked like he'd been run over by a truck.

REESE

I did NOT feel good at breakfast that day. I thought I was going to pass out into my cereal.

REESE AT BREAKFAST
(artist's re-creation)
(artist = Claudia)

CLAUDIA

Bet-wise, I wasn't sure if Reese's situation was good or bad for me. On the one hand, it meant he couldn't post any more Blurts that might go viral. But on the other hand, he also couldn't post any more Blurts that'd drive his followers away like rats fleeing a sinking ship.

19,046 FOLLOWERS

REESE:
↓ 6,000 followers
in 4 days

Either way, though, I was feeling good about my odds. I'd gotten almost 600 more followers overnight, and my best Blurts hadn't even posted yet.

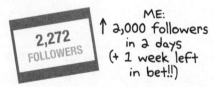

2,272 FOLLOWERS

ME:
↑ 2,000 followers
in 2 days
(+ 1 week left
in bet!!)

I was especially excited about #13, which I was going to put up right after school.

STILL FRAMES FROM <u>FURRY MENACE</u> #13:

Jens
steals
bat from
me...

...and I pull knife on Jens (FYI knife was fake)
(from costume store)

NOT
PICTURED:
Jens drops bat
and runs away

When I got to school, there was serious
buzz in the cafeteria about *The Furry Menace*.

SOPHIE

It was like that first morning after
Reese's Blurt posted. EVERYBODY was watching
your Blurts. And they loved them!

JENS

My friends say to me things like,
"DOOOOOD, these Blurts are off a hook!"

And the pain on my head was gone by
then. So I start to think, "After all, maybe
this was good to do."

JAMES

I was really tempted to out myself as the director. It was so annoying having to listen to people talk about how crazy your imaginary cousin was. That was MY crazy!

CLAUDIA

The absolutely best part of that morning was watching Athena and the Fembots react to the Blurts.

PARVATI

Can I just say, it was HILARIOUS when Athena accused you of cheating?

She was like, "You can't post Blurts that aren't you!"

And you were like, "That's me in the Flubby costume!"

And she was like, "YOU CAN'T BE A FLUBBY!"

CARMEN

So you took out the rules Toby typed up and you were like, "I don't see anything in here about Flubbies."

And the whole cafeteria was like, "You lose, Athena!"

The look on her face after that was SO GREAT.

CLAUDIA

Athena was so furious that she and the other Fembots spent the rest of the day trying to shame me for looking overweight in the Flubby costume.

ATHENA

Excuse me, but I was just stating a fact. I mean, it's, like, BEYOND obvious you don't care about your appearance. But tbh? That costume was NOT flattering. You looked like a blue cow.

PARVATI

Ugh! I hate Athena so much. When she and Meredith and Ling "moo'd" at you after third period? DISGUSTING.

CLAUDIA

It really was. But it also felt like a victory. Athena was clearly lashing out because she was worried she was going to lose the bet.

Also, FYI, that costume was padded. But even if it wasn't, no one should EVER have to feel uncomfortable in their own body. Even a Flubby body. Making people feel bad about the way they look is just totally wrong and evil.

WE ARE ALL PERFECT JUST THE WAY WE ARE
(even murderous psycho Flubbies)

But the Flubby-shaming just made me even more psyched to come home after school and post more Blurts. When I checked the app from my phone on the bus home from school, I was at 2,600 followers, and *The Furry Menace* #6 had racked up over 150,000 Blips.

Considering how awesome and hilarious Blurts #13–16 were, I felt sure my numbers were about to take off like a rocket. I was so excited that when I got home, I didn't even stop in the kitchen for a snack. I went straight to my bedroom to post *The Furry Menace* #13 from my laptop.

And that's when I realized something had gone horribly, terribly wrong.

Blurts #1 through 12 had all disappeared from my page. In their place was this ugly black box:

ASHLEY

I seriously have NEVER heard a human being scream that loud in my life. I was in the kitchen when I heard you, and all I could think was, "Claude has DEFINITELY cut off all her fingers. Or maybe her whole hand."

CLAUDIA

By the time Ashley got to my bedroom,

I'd found the notice from Blurt Legal in my
Direct Messages:

**@BLURTLEGAL TO @CLAUDAROO (Blurt Direct
Message)**

ATTENTION

We have received a trademark infringement complaint
regarding a Blurt(s) you posted, as follows:

**Complaint from Children's Television Laboratory regarding
inappropriate use of trademarked content FLUBBY™
CHARACTER COSTUME**

Blurt ID: kzVj235x2	Blurt ID: zjKm875m1
Blurt ID: xrDu733j6	Blurt ID: ptMI673d2
Blurt ID: abEq098p5	Blurt ID: plTr473v1
Blurt ID: rtUs324i6	Blurt ID: lbVm385t9
Blurt ID: gbZf384d3	Blurt ID: xlFt890b4
Blurt ID: mdGi682e1	Blurt ID: ipZw190d8

*ALL
OF MY
→FURRY
MENACE
BLURTS*

**Further incidents of trademark infringement will result in the
deletion of your account. Please delete any Blurts for which
you have not obtained the necessary rights and refrain from
posting future Blurts containing unlicensed material.**

**If your Blurt(s) has been misrepresented, you may submit
a counter-notification. Be aware that under section
512(c) of the Digital Millennium Copyright Act, willful
misrepresentation may expose you to civil liability for
damages suffered by the rights holder.**

The Blurt Legal Department

CLAUDIA

The first thing I did was contact a lawyer.

CLAUDIA AND DAD (text messages)

> DAD MAJOR EMERGENCY PLS
> CHECK YR EMAIL ASAP

Are you ok??????

> HAVING PANIC ATTACK
>
> CHECK EMAIL

Breathe into a paper bag

> THAT DOESN'T WORK
>
> CHECK YR EMAIL!!!

Just did

> WHAT DOES THIS MEAN?
>
> CAN I STILL POST MY BLURTS?

Calling you now

CLAUDIA

When he called, Dad was VERY kind and supportive. Which I realize was not easy, because I was basically a hot mess. And it took him a while to calm me down.

So as a parent, he was totally awesome.

But as a lawyer, I was VERY disappointed in him.

Because what I really needed him to do was to sue somebody and/or get a judge to issue a court order so I could keep posting *Furry Menace* Blurts.

And he basically took the Children's Television Laboratory's side.

ERIC S. TAPPER (aka "DAD"), father/lawyer of Claudia

The law's the law, kiddo. And let me tell you, the Children's Television Lab is AGGRESSIVE in protecting their trademarks. If they don't want Flubby™ going on a crazy homicidal rampage, he's not going. End of story.

But I have to say—as a parent, I'm incredibly proud of you. There aren't too many 12-year-olds out there who've gotten a cease and desist order

TM = trademark (Dad says to be on legal safe side, I have to use this when talking about Flubby™ from now on)

from a major corporation. That's a real
accomplishment.

CLAUDIA

    Thanks, Dad. Sorry about all the crying
in the middle of your work day.

DAD

    Don't sweat it, kiddo. That's what I'm
here for.

CHAPTER 17
NEVER GIVE YOUR PASSWORD
TO XANDER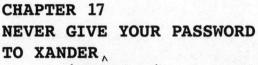
(OR ANYBODY)
(BUT ESPECIALLY
XANDER)

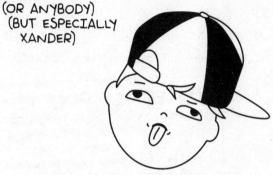

CLAUDIA

While the Children's Television Lab was ruining my entire Blurt strategy, Xander was busy ruining Reese's entire life.

REESE

He didn't ruin my WHOLE life. Just some parts of it.

CLAUDIA

Whatever. You still shouldn't have given him your Blurt password.

XANDER

I coulda guessed it, yo. Bruh's password wuz "password"!

REESE

It wasn't "password"! It was "Password123"!
And "Password" was capitalized!

CLAUDIA

Wow, Reese. That is just...REALLY not smart.

INTERNET PRO TIP:
DO NOT MAKE YOUR PASSWORD
"PASSWORD" (or anything else
that's super easy to guess)
(other bad passwords include:
your name, your pet's name,
your birthday, 123456, etc.)

REESE

I know! Okay? Geez! Just let me tell the
story.

So after our last couple Blurts had
crashed and burned, Xander figured out the
way to get huge was to do a collab with a
famous Blurt star.

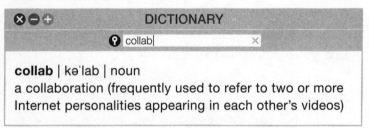

DICTIONARY

collab

collab | kə'lab | noun
a collaboration (frequently used to refer to two or more
Internet personalities appearing in each other's videos)

XANDER

   Collabs is where it's at! If
Skronkmonster did a collab with BewBewBoy,
we'd get dem twenty million BewBewBoy
eyeballs on us!

REESE

   It seemed like a really good idea.

CLAUDIA

   For YOU, sure. But not for BewBewBoy.
Because he had A THOUSAND TIMES as many
followers as you did. So there was literally
nothing in it for him.

REESE

   Do you want me to tell the story? Or do
you just want to make me feel bad?

CLAUDIA

   I'm sorry. Keep going.

REESE

   So Xander DM'ed BewBewBoy to see if he
was up for a collab.

Xander's 1st DM
to BewBewBoy

@SKRONKMONSTER _ X TO @BEWBEWBOY (Blurt DM)

WUT UP BEWBEWBOY???

WANT 2 DO A COLLAB W @SKRONKMONSTER???

ITD B EPIC CUZ WE R BOTH METAWORLD/BLURT STARS

WE CAN THROW U OF A CLIFF IN A DEATHMATCH

OR U CAN THROW US OFF

EITHER WAY ITD B EPIC!!!!!!!

HIT US BACK N SAY WHEN U CAN DO IT W R FREE 4-10PM TMW

REESE

    I was hyped to do it. BewBewBoy's my idol!

    But he didn't answer. So Xander DM'ed him again.

    And he still didn't answer.

    Then Xander DM'ed him, like, ten more times.

Xander's 14th DM to BewBewBoy (in one day)

@SKRONKMONSTER _ X TO @BEWBEWBOY (Blurt DM)

WUTS UR PROBLEM BRUH?

R U SCARED @SKRONKMONSTER WILL KICK UR BUTT????

I BET U R

IF U DONT COLLAB W US U R A WUSS!!!!!!!

REESE

Then BewBewBoy blocked Xander, so he couldn't send any more DMs.

And Xander got seriously grumpfed. He was all, "Let's just kick his butt without him!!!!"

I didn't really think that was possible. 'Cause if you're going to kick somebody's butt, it seems like their butt has to BE there.

But Xander was like, "We'll fake him."

And he created this MetaWorld account called ".BewBewBoy." Then he made the avatar look EXACTLY like BewBewBoy's avatar. note added period

ACTUAL BEWBEWBOY   XANDER'S FAKE
                         BEWBEWBOY

The idea was that I'd kill the fake
BewBewBoy in a deathmatch, and I'd Blurt that
and be like, "I KICKED BEWBEWBOY'S BUTT!"

But I wasn't really into doing it. I
mean, if somebody made a fake Skronkmonster,
and killed him, and then Blurted that they'd
kicked MY butt? I'd be all kinds of mad.

Plus by then, Mom and Dad had taken
all my electronics away. So I told Xander I
couldn't do it, 'cause I couldn't go online.

And he was like, "No worries. Just gimme
your password."

Then Xander logged in as me and got Wyatt
to be the fake BewBewBoy.

WYATT

I didn't think it was a good idea, either.
'Cause I was worried if I pretended to be
BewBewBoy, all his Bewbees would come after me.

REESE

The Bewbees are this huge group of
BewBewBoy fans. They're kind of like an online
gang. And they're pretty scary. Like, if you ever
say anything bad about BewBewBoy in a comment
section, the Bewbees will come at you HARD.

Plus a bunch of them are hackers. So
they know how to doxx people.

DICTIONARY

doxx

doxx | däks | verb
to obtain personal information (such as a person's
physical address, phone number, photograph, etc.) and
then broadcast it via the Internet, often for the purpose
of harassment, intimidation, or revenge.

Which means they can actually mess with
you in real life. Not just online.

CLAUDIA
If you're reading this and wondering,
"Is Xander about to enrage a giant army
of evil trolls with terrifying powers who
will descend on my brother and attempt to
destroy him by any means possible?" the
answer is YES.

REESE
Who's telling the story here, Claudia?

CLAUDIA
Sorry! Go on.

REESE

Xander told Wyatt there was no way
the Bewbees could trace the .BewBewBoy
account back to him. So Wyatt was like,
"Fine."

And they made this Blurt of me killing
BewBewBoy. Except it wasn't me, and it wasn't
BewBewBoy. Then they Blurted it from my
Skronkmonster account.

BEWBEWBOY GETTIN' PWNED!!!

Just to make sure BewBewBoy and the
Bewbees all saw it, Xander tagged a bunch
of them in the comment section.

BLURT COMMENT SECTION

XANDER

I ain't sayin' it was a good idea.
But that Blurt wuz gettin MAD Blips at
the beginning! Tons of eyeballs on that
bad boy!

REESE

Yeah—from people who all wanted to
kill me after they saw it!

XANDER

I ain't sayin' it was a good idea! I'm
just sayin' it wuz popular.

Plus, I ain't the one with dem baby-weak
passwords.

384 comments [load more]

@AllHailBewBew Wow @Skronkmonster U have a deathwish????

@BewBewsArmy ITS ON NOW

@BewBee_1000 LET THE DOXXING BEGIN

@TheMightyBew this iz gonna hurt

@BewBeeTheFirst SAY BYE BYE TO UR LIFE @Skronkmonster

@AllHailBewBew OMG its too easy! His password is Password123!!!!!!!!

@BewBee_1000 smh

@AllHailBewBew IM IN GOT ALL HIS INFO POSTING ON CHAN NOW

@TheMightyBew let's do this

@TheBewIsMyShepherd TOTAL DESTRUCTION OF @Skronkmonster IN 5...4...3...

CHAPTER 18
I PIN ALL MY HOPES
ON SOME FRENCH GUY

CLAUDIA

While Xander was setting my brother's life on fire, I was trying desperately to come up with another way to beat Athena.

(not literally) (but close)

At first, I was hoping James could redo the *Furry Menace* Blurts with a cartoon character who wouldn't sue me for turning him/her/it into a homicidal maniac.

CLAUDIA AND JAMES (text messages)

> What if I get Elmo costume and we reshoot?

> Elmo lawyers r prob worse than Flubby™ lawyers

> Then what?

I got nothing. And I have to stop helping u

Too much heat and I cant afford another lawsuit

What do you mean "another" lawsuit?

NM. Going underground

Pls delete these texts and lose this number

CLAUDIA

That was Thursday night. On Friday morning, I woke up with a stomachache (other 5% = bad turkey dog from Thurs. dinner) that I am 95% sure was stress-related.

And it only got worse when I went to school. The Fembots were so excited to taunt me that they were practically peeing their pants.

SOPHIE

Is it just me, or were Clarissa and Ling waiting at the front door so they could sing "YOU'RE SOOOOO DOOMED!" at you the second you walked in?

CLAUDIA

Yeah, they were pretty much stalking me.
So I had to hide out in the library again.

Parvati met me there, and we went into
library Narnia to discuss my absolutely last
hope for victory: BlurtUp.

PARVATI

At that point, BlurtUp was happening
in exactly 29 hours and 43 minutes. I knew
this because my official BlurtUp app had a
countdown clock.

AND I COULDN'T WAIT TO MEET TYLER PURDY
BECAUSE I AM HIS NUMBER ONE FANGIRL OF ALL
TIME! AAAAAAAAH!

Also, I was totally sure Marcel would
be your knight in shining armor and save
you from the Fembots.

CLAUDIA

I decided to do what Parvati had been
telling me to do all week: go to the BlurtUp
festival, somehow meet Marcel Mourlot, and
convince him to Reblurt "Windmill" to his
30,000,000 followers.

Tbh, I am so clueless when it comes to
Blurt stars that if it weren't for Parvati,

I wouldn't even have known Marcel was the best one to ask for an RB.

PARVATI

Marcel was perfect! He's INCREDIBLY supportive of his fans, and he's constantly RB'ing them to help make their dreams come true. Like, I don't think Brian Messer would even BE a star today if Marcel hadn't RB'ed him so much.

Reblurted by TheRealMarcel
BrianMesser

12,942,714 BLIPS

BOOTY WHAP! (click link for video!!!)

943 comments [load more]

@TheRealMarcel I THINK @BrianMesser IS AMAZING HE IS ONLY 17 BUT SO WISE AND HIS SONG "BOOTY WHAP" WILL CHANGE THE WORLD CHECK IT OUT ON MEVID!!!!

And I was SO EXCITED for you that you were coming to BlurtUp! Once Marcel RB'ed you, not only would you beat Athena, but "Windmill" would FINALLY be a hit! It was going to be totally life-changing for you!

I was also excited for me. Because it seemed like it'd be way better to go with your dad than my dad.

CLAUDIA

Parvati's dad was originally going to take her to BlurtUp. But he's a doctor, and he was on call that day. Which meant Parvati might have to leave BlurtUp early if someone needed an emergency orthopedist.

So she wanted to trade up to a parent who wouldn't mess up her chances of meeting Tyler Purdy. And because Parvati's mom had to take Akash to a robotics fair in Scarsdale that day, and my mom is very crafty about avoiding things she doesn't want to do, my dad wound up taking us.

MOM AND DAD (text messages)

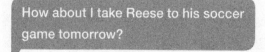

Great!

Excellent. U just have to hang out w Claudia and Parvati

Maybe I'll take them to a movie

You're taking them to BlurtUp

What on earth is that?

Hard to explain. Try googling it

NOOOOOOOOOOO

CLAUDIA

Unfortunately for both me and Parvati, even though my dad is not a doctor on call, he IS a lawyer with an evil boss. So Dad wound up having to do a bunch of work at home on Saturday morning before we could leave. And we got started a LOT later than Parvati wanted to.

PARVATI

Claude, you know I love your dad...and I was fine with us not camping out overnight, because I totally get that it's illegal to do that and we couldn't get in line before 5:00am anyway...but we DEFINITELY should've been there by 5:00am LATEST.

CLAUDIA

I know! I just couldn't make it happen. To be fair, we DID get there half an hour before the gates opened at noon.

PARVATI

Yeah—along with the gazillion other girls who were ahead of us!

Which is why we had to totally change our whole strategy for getting Marcel to Reblurt you and Tyler to fall in love with me.

CLAUDIA

Parvati's original plan was to get to BlurtUp so early that we'd be able to snag a spot right in front of the stage, where A) I could hand Marcel a thumb drive with the "Windmill" video on it, and B) Parvati could make eye contact with Tyler Purdy long enough for him to realize she was his soul mate.

But even though we ran for the stage as soon as the gates opened, this was as close as we could get:

THE CLOSEST WE COULD GET TO BLURTUP STAGE:

Which was not close at all.

So we decided to switch from a "Stage" strategy to a "Meet and Greet" strategy.

Basically, BlurtUp had two parts. There was the stage, where all of the Blurt stars did their thing—like singing, or rapping, or just standing there and being cute. And then there was the Meet and Greet tent, where you could actually meet and/or take selfies with all the Blurt stars.

If you had a $500 "VIP Platinum" or a $350 "VIP Gold" ticket, you were guaranteed to get into the tent and meet all the stars.

Needless to say, Parvati and I did not have those. We also did not have $100 "VIP Bronze" tickets, which guaranteed you'd get into the tent, but NOT necessarily meet everybody.

What we had were $30 "Not Any Kind Of VIP At All" tickets. Which guaranteed nothing, except that if you stood around outside the tent long enough, one of the stars MIGHT come out of the tent for 30 seconds and take a selfie with you.

ATHENA, the most evil person in the world

Ohmygosh, did you not have VIP status? So you and Poverty were, like, stuck in the middle of that sad crowd of desperate girls standing outside the Meet and Greet tent like homeless people?

Athena's totally disgusting nickname for Parvati

SARCASM → That is the saddest thing EVER! I am SO sorry! If it makes you feel better, I'll let you reprint my ClickChat photo of Tyler Purdy hugging me for your little book.

ARTIST'S RE-CREATION OF ATHENA'S CLICKCHAT PHOTO WITH TYLER PURDY (she wanted $500 for rights to use actual pic)

CLAUDIA

 (also sarcasm)

That's SO nice of you, Athena! But I think I'd rather just claw my eyes out with a fork.

PARVATI

Can I just say, there is NO WAY Tyler enjoyed that hug? You could practically SEE the pain in his eyes in that pic. ATHENA IS NOT SPECIAL TO HIM!!!!

CLAUDIA

Long story short, we spent our first two hours at BlurtUp standing in the crowd outside the Meet and Greet tent and waiting for a miracle. Which, BTW, my dad thought was insane. He kept saying things like, "Don't you want to go back to the stage and watch the whoever-they-ares do their whatever-they-do?"

crowd outside Meet + Greet tent

PARVATI

Your dad totally did not get the deal with BlurtUp.

But can I just say, I never had any doubt that a miracle would happen? Because

visualization is a very powerful tool. And
I was using ALL my mental brainpower to
visualize Tyler coming out of the tent and
seeing me.

Plus I was holding up my sign. So when
Tyler DID come out, he'd see me and come over.

PARVATI'S SIGN

CLAUDIA

I have to admit that after two hours, I
was starting to agree with Dad that we were
out of our minds to think standing outside
the Meet and Greet tent was a good idea.
That whole two hours, the only Blurt star
who came out of the tent was so minor-league
I can't even remember his name.

PARVATI

    Joey Buffata.

CLAUDIA

    Whatever. But here is the amazing
thing: two hours into our wait, TYLER
PURDY ACTUALLY CAME OUT OF THE TENT!

    When he did, everybody in the crowd
started to scream at once. And I think
Tyler must have seen Parvati's gigantic
sign because he started moving in our
direction.

PARVATI

    I couldn't believe it. My whole
body started shaking. And there were,
like, serious fireworks exploding in
my brain.

CLAUDIA

    I could tell something epic was about
to happen, so I turned away for a second
to get my phone out and capture the moment
when Tyler came through the crowd and gave
Parvati a big hug, or stared into her eyes,
or took her backstage to eat strawberries,
or whatever.

But when I turned back to Parvati with my camera ready, she'd already fainted.

THE MOMENT I TURNED BACK TO PARVATI:

Tyler

crowd
(screaming
for Tyler)

Dad (freaking out)

Parvati (fainted)

CHAPTER 19
THE BLOWUP AT BLURTUP

CLAUDIA

When Parvati fainted, there were a lot of screaming girls in between her and Tyler. So I am honestly not sure if he ever knew Parvati had passed out at the sight of him.

If he did, though, he is the worst person on earth. Because if someone holding a poster saying I was their soul mate passed out at the sight of ME, I would at least autograph the poster for her.

By the time Parvati came to, Tyler was gone. And other than being really mad that she'd missed him, she seemed mostly fine. But the BlurtUp security people still insisted on calling an ambulance.

This is not as dramatic as it sounds, because the ambulance was a golf cart.

BLURTUP AMBULANCE (pretty lame)

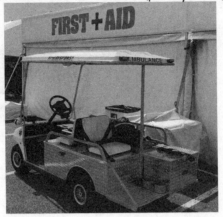

ATHENA, pure evil in human form

A golf cart??? That is SO basic! If I'D
passed out? With my VIP Platinum ticket?
They would have airlifted me to safety in a
helicopter.

CLAUDIA

Thanks for your input, Athena.

The golf cart ambulance drove Parvati
to the first aid tent, where the BlurtUp

prob ⟶ medical people made her lie down for a while
not real
doctors and drink orange juice.
(might've
been
college **PARVATI**
kids?)
They wouldn't let me leave for half an
hour. Which was totally ridiculous! I was

fine! I mean, Tyler was already gone from the Meet and Greet. And it wasn't like Cody and Cody were going to make me faint.

BTW, I hope my dad didn't get too mad at your dad when he found out about the fainting.

CLAUDIA

Don't worry about it. My dad's a lawyer, so he's used to having people get mad at him.

DAD EXPLAINS TO MR. GUPTA THAT
HIS DAUGHTER JUST FAINTED

PARVATI NOT sarcasm
(Parvati felt v. bad about this)

And I am SO SORRY you had to leave the Meet and Greet line before you had a chance to give the thumb drive to Marcel!

CLAUDIA

It's fine. I'm pretty sure Marcel never even came out of the Meet and Greet tent anyway.

By the time Parvati got the all clear from the doctor/college kid in the medical tent, it was just five minutes before Marcel Mourlot was due on stage. So we ran to the stage area, then wormed our way through the crowd to get as close as we possibly could to the front.

Which, again, was not very close at all.

So when Marcel came on stage, I knew there was no chance I was ever going to get close enough to hand him the thumb drive with the "Windmill" video on it.

PARVATI

You were freaking out because we were so far away from Marcel.

But then I pointed out that even though you were too far away to HAND the thumb drive to him, you were definitely close enough to THROW it to him.

CLAUDIA

This was true.

Probably. I actually wasn't sure. Because even though the thumb drive was very easy to throw, I am not exactly the world's greatest thrower.

But it wasn't like I had a choice. If I didn't throw it, I had zero chance of ever getting it to Marcel.

And when Marcel said to the crowd, "OKAAAY, NOW I AM GOING TO SING ZEE FUNNY ZEBRA SONG...." I realized it was now or never. Because once he started the zebra song (whatever that was), I'd never get his attention.

MOMENTS BEFORE I THREW THUMB DRIVE

Marcel (behind selfie stick)

no idea whose head this is (maybe one of the Codys?)

So I screamed "MARCEL, CATCH THIS!" as loud as I could.

Then I threw the thumb drive at the stage.

Like I said, I'm not a great thrower. So I didn't even think I'd get it close to Marcel.

And I absolutely, positively DID NOT MEAN TO HIT HIM IN THE EYE.

If I'd had ANY idea that might happen, I NEVER would've used a thumb drive with pointy Batman ears.

I SHOULD _NOT_ HAVE USED JAMES'S POINTY-EARED THUMB DRIVE

PARVATI

OMG, it was terrifying. Marcel, like, fell to his knees and started holding his eye and screaming in French.

And right away, all his fans started looking around like, "WHO DID THAT? AND HOW CAN WE KILL THEM?"

CLAUDIA

Parvati said, "We need to get out of here STAT."

I agreed. So we grabbed my dad and ran for the subway.

I was so scared we were going to get chased down by angry Marcel fans that my heart didn't stop pounding until we were on the 7 train heading back into Manhattan.

Which was when Mom texted Dad that Reese was in serious trouble.

DAD AND MOM (text messages)

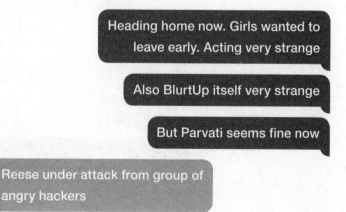

Heading home now. Girls wanted to leave early. Acting very strange

Also BlurtUp itself very strange

But Parvati seems fine now

Reese under attack from group of angry hackers

Huh??

Started when my mother called

Wanting to know why her grandson emailed her photo of a dog pooping on his head

Are you sure R didn't do that?

Dog pooping photo went to his entire address book

Including Principal Spooner and all his teachers

OMG calling you now

Reese can't log in to his email

Hackers in control of it

Also his Blurt and ClickChat accts

Why won't you answer phone?

On other line trying to fix pizza problem

Pizza problem?

Someone keeps sending us pizzas

From 9 different pizza places so far

Wait doorman just buzzed

Make that 10

Coming home ASAP

And now the police are here

CHAPTER 20
REESE GETS
CRUSHED
BY THE
BEWBEE ARMY

CLAUDIA

By the time we got home from BlurtUp, the police had left. Mom said they were very polite, but it was still extremely scary to have them show up at the door because an anonymous caller had tipped them off that Reese was behind a whole bunch of armed robberies.

VIEW FROM THE FRONT DOOR WHEN COPS ARRIVED
(artist's re-creation)

REESE

It was totally cray! I mean, I knew the
Bewbees were coming at me hard by then. But
I didn't think it was gonna be "the cops are
here" hard.

CLAUDIA

When did you first realize the Bewbees
were attacking you?

REESE

I guess at the soccer game that
morning. We were warming up, and Xander
was like, "Yo, why'd you change your Blurt
password?"

And I was like, "I didn't."

And he was like, "SOMEBODY did."

So I knew something was up. And after
the game, I asked Mom if I could have my
phone back for a couple minutes to make sure
there wasn't anything wrong with my Blurt
account.

When I turned the phone on, the first
thing I saw was a text from Wyatt.

WYATT AND REESE (Text messages copied from Reese's phone)

OMG I CANT BELEVE YOU POSTED THAT!!!

> Posted what

THE DOG POOPING ON YOUR HEAD

> What r u talking about

YOUR CLICKCHAT POST

Y DID U EMAIL IT, TOO??????

REESE

I tried to open ClickChat, but the app was like, "Incorrect password."

Which was scary. I couldn't get into my own account! And the Blurt app was the same way.

So I was already starting to freak out when Grandma called. And all of a sudden, Mom was like, "REESE! WHY DID YOU EMAIL AN OBSCENE PHOTO TO YOUR GRANDMOTHER???"

Then Mom checked HER email and was like, "I GOT IT, TOO!!"

CLAUDIA

Which photo was it? The dog?

REESE

One of the dogs, yeah. I mean, eventually, there were, like, ten different dog photos flying around the Internet. But all of them used the exact same pic of my head from that soccer photo the Bewbees got off my ClickChat feed.

CLAUDIA

And the dogs were all pooping on your head?

DOG PHOTO (#3 of 10+) (original photo had actual pic of Reese's head, not cartoon)

REESE

Not exactly. My head WAS the poop. So
they weren't pooping ON me. They were just...
pooping me.

And it wasn't just dogs. They used
a bunch of other animals. Cows, horses,
elephants...that rhinoceros...

Hey, wait a minute—you're not putting
those pics in the book, are you?

RHINOCEROS PHOTO (w/cartoon head added)

CLAUDIA

I kind of have to.

REESE

NO, YOU DON'T!

CLAUDIA

Yes, I do! This book's all about the bad things that can happen if you're not careful about what you do online. So I think people need to see the actual photos to really understand the dangers here.

REESE

Can't you just SAY they were crazy bad? Do you have to show them, too?

CLAUDIA

How about I draw a picture of your head and Photoshop it over the actual heads so the dogs are just pooping a cartoon head?

REESE

I guess that's okay. Just don't make the cartoon look too much like me.

DOG PHOTO
(#7 of 10+)
(this one was my favorite)
(because the dog is smiling)

CLAUDIA

Deal. Where were we?

REESE

Let's see...locked out of my accounts...
the pics of dogs pooping out my head got
sent to everybody on earth...the pizzas
started showing up...then the cops came.

But honestly? The cops weren't THAT bad.
'Cause once they figured out they'd been
pranked by hackers, they put me on some list
so they wouldn't have to keep showing
up whenever the hackers called in a
fake tip.

also now we are on "do-not-deliver" list with every pizza place on Upper West Side ⌣

I think the worst part was what
happened to me on MetaWorld. The Bewbees
took over my account, and by the time I
got it back, they'd stolen all my goldz,
killed all my soldiers, and burned down
my castle.

goldz = MetaWorld money

Plus they figured out what servers I
like to play on and started stalking me.
So whenever I'd log on to play a deathmatch,
I'd get gang-murdered in the first five
seconds.

That was definitely the worst.

CLAUDIA

I think Mom and Dad would disagree.
They'd probably say the worst part was the
hours and hours they had to spend trying to
get all your accounts back.

Plus the fact that now when you google
"Reese Tapper," all that comes up are
pictures of animals pooping out your head.

That's not going to look good when you
grow up and try to get a job.

REESE

I guess not. But I feel like I've got a few years to turn it around.

CLAUDIA

All in all, the Bewbees' attack on Reese was devastating. Even weeks later, Mom, Dad, and Reese were STILL trying to fix all the problems it caused.

On a personal level, I spent the whole rest of that weekend freaking out. This was partly because Reese is my brother. And even though he can be seriously annoying, it's very scary to see bad things happen to him.

But it was also because I was terrified that an angry mob of Marcel Mourlot fans were about to launch EXACTLY the same kind of attack on me.

CHAPTER 21
MARKED FOR DEATH
BY THE LOVEFIGHTERS

CLAUDIA

Even though the major issue in our apartment for pretty much the whole 24 hours after we got home from BlurtUp was the attack on Reese, I couldn't stop thinking about the fact that I'd accidentally hit Marcel Mourlot in the eye with an extremely pointy thumb drive.

I was VERY worried he might be badly hurt. And I was equally worried I might have committed a crime, and the cops were going to put out a warrant for my arrest.

So the first thing I did when the Reese-related insanity settled down was to go online and check Marcel's Blurt page.

Fortunately, he'd already Blurted that he was fine. Or at least not permanently injured.

MARCEL'S BLURT: "My cornea eez scratched,
but my heart eez fuuuull!

TheRealMarcel   1,485,399 BLIPS

DONT WORRY ITS JUST A SCRATCH!!!!

2,743 comments [load more]

@TheRealMarcel NYC LOVEFIGHTERS I M SO SORRY I HAD TO
LEAVE THE STAGE EARLY!!! I HAVE A SCRATCH CORNEA BUT
IT SHOULD BE OK IN A WEEK SO I WILL SEE U ALL AT BLURTUP
CHICAGO NEXT SAT!!!

This was a huge relief. But it was also
confusing. For one thing, I had no idea what
"Lovefighters" were.

PARVATI
    OMG, Claude—how could you follow Marcel

on Blurt and not know what Lovefighters
are?! They're his superfans! They call
themselves Lovefighters because Marcel says
love is the most important thing in the
world. And if you want it, you have to fight
for it.

Or something like that.

CLAUDIA

So Lovefighters are like the Marcel
Mourlot version of Bewbees?

PARVATI

Eeew! What's a Bewbee? That sounds
totally gross.

CLAUDIA

Never mind.

When I first saw Marcel's Blurt, I
thought I was in the clear. Because not only
was he only a little bit hurt, but it seemed
like he wasn't going to press charges.

But then I started reading the comment
section. And that's when I realized the
Lovefighters were out for blood.

Specifically, MY blood.

2,743 comments [load more]

@AnnieGrz **OMG MARCEL U R SO BRAVE**

@luvfitr100 **WE HAVE TO FIND WHO DID THIS**

@emilyhenk **Marcel must be avanged!!!!!!!** ⚔ ⚔ ⚔

@NJLoveFighter **I WAS THERE I GOT A PIC OF IT**

@emilyhenk **Pic of what I don't see anything**

@NJLoveFighter **IF U BLOW IT UP U CAN SEE SOMETHING FLYING THRU THE AIR TOWARD STAGE**

@MarcelLoveFighter **This is brilliant!! We can track down the evil scum w our selfies!**

@lil.neenzas **everybody who was there post ur pics!!!!!**

@MarcelLoveFighter **GO LOVEFIGHTERS We r going to crowdsource this hatr and destroy him**

CLAUDIA

When I saw this, I practically had a
heart attack. Seeing as how EVERY SINGLE
PERSON at BlurtUp was holding a camera phone
and pointing it at the stage when I threw
the thumb drive, it seemed like it was only

a matter of time before somebody posted a
pic that totally busted me.

I spent all of Sunday refreshing the
comment section every two minutes and
watching the Lovefighters get closer and
closer to revealing my true identity.

BLURT COMMENT SECTION

2,743 comments [load more]

@FlorisDiz u guys I think this is her

definitely my head

@luvfitr100 omg I cant believe its a girl

@NJLoveFighter EVERYBODY SEARCH YOUR PICS FOR DARK HAIRED GIRL AT BLURTUP NYC

@FormrBlbr Ummmmm…Thats most girls at BlurtUp NYC

@FlorisDiz she has navy blue shirt long sleeve

@FlorisDiz also wearing skirt w black n white pattern:

(now I CAN'T EVER WEAR THIS SKIRT AGAIN)

@NJLoveFighter LOVEFIGHTERS LETS DO THIS!!!!!

@MarcelLoveFighter Yes!!!!! We r going to make her pay!!!

CLAUDIA

I was so scared about the Lovefighters coming after me that when Carmen messaged me on Sunday afternoon, I'd almost forgotten about my bet with Athena.

CARMEN AND CLAUDIA (ClickChat Direct Messenger)

Carmen

me

CONGRATS!!!

On what

REESES BLURT ACCOUNT GOT DELETED
SO U WIN THE BET RIGHT???

CHAPTER 22
I SNATCH VICTORY FROM
THE JAWS OF DEFEAT

CLAUDIA

First of all, it was news to me that Reese's Blurt account had been completely deleted.

REESE

Me too. The Bewbees must've posted a bunch of really skeezy stuff on my page because Blurt shut my whole account down. The same thing happened to my ClickChat account, and it took Dad a CRAZY amount of time to get ClickChat to reopen it.

After that, he was like, "How bad do you want your Blurt account back? 'Cause I'm REALLY getting sick of waiting on hold for two hours to talk to tech support."

And I was like, "You know what? Just
forget about it."

Because by then, I was kind of wishing
I'd never even heard of Blurt.

CLAUDIA

When I found out Reese's account was
gone, the first thing I did was take a very
close look at the original bet that Athena
and I had agreed to.

All it said was this:

THE BET

ATHENA BETS CLAUDIA THAT BY THE TIME SCHOOL ENDS AT 2:55PM ON THURSDAY
THE 26TH, REESE (@SKRONKMONSTER) WILL HAVE MORE BLURT FOLLOWERS THAN
CLAUDIA (@CLAUDAROO).

...and this:

RULES

REESE CAN'T CHEAT OR SET HIS ACCOUNT TO PRIVATE OR DO ANYTHING ELSE TO HELP
HIS SISTER WIN OR SHE WILL AUTOMATICALLY LOSE.

What it did NOT say was ANYTHING
about what would happen if Blurt deleted
Reese's account because hackers had taken
it over and Blurted a bunch of incredibly
inappropriate clips. (not sure what the clips were,
but prob totally filthy)

So I spent the rest of Sunday doing two things: A) constantly refreshing the comment section of Marcel's Blurt to see if the Lovefighters had figured out who I was, and B) getting ready for a MAJOR argument in the cafeteria on Monday morning.

Because I knew Athena wasn't going to give up without a fight.

SOPHIE

It was actually an interesting question. "If an account gets deleted, how many followers does it have?"

It's kind of like, "If a tree falls in the forest and nobody's around, does it make a sound?"

PARVATI

Hello? OF COURSE it makes a sound! And OF COURSE Claudia won the bet! If your account disappears, so do your followers!

CLAUDIA

In the end, Reese's friend Wyatt came up with the key piece of evidence for my argument.

WYATT

I didn't get on Blurt until after the bet started. So I was only following six people.

And after Reese's account got deleted, my home page said I was only following FIVE people. And Reese wasn't one of them.

WYATT'S BLURT PAGE

0	2	⑤
POSTS	FOLLOWERS	FOLLOWING

CLAUDIA

In other words, Wyatt and all the other 19,000 people who were following Reese had automatically UN-followed him when Blurt deleted his account.

So if his account was reactivated, it would have zero followers.

Which meant I won.

ATHENA, the bride of Satan

I'm sorry, but that is the dumbest, lamest thing I have EVER heard.

CLAUDIA

The rest of the sixth grade didn't think so.

ATHENA

Because they are idiots.

CARMEN

That whole scene in the cafeteria
was SO great. Like, when Athena claimed
Reese got Blurt to delete his account on
purpose?

REESE

I was like, "Do you seriously think I
sent a picture of myself getting pooped out
by a dog to EVERYBODY ON EARTH just to help
my sister? I don't even like her that much!!"
No offense, Claudia.

CLAUDIA

It's fine. It was actually very helpful
that you said that.

It was also helpful that I wasn't trying
to claim Athena owed me $1,000. I didn't want
her money—I just wanted the whole thing to
be over. So all I did was argue that nobody
won and the bet should be called off.

And when Athena said that was ridiculous,
I asked for a show of hands from everybody
in the cafeteria.

CARMEN

You were like, "Raise your hand if you think the bet should be off." And pretty much everybody in the cafeteria raised their hands except for Athena and the Fembots.

Then Athena called us all idiots and stormed out of the room. It was so awesome.

CLAUDIA

It really was. And it would have been a great ending...if it was actually the end of the story.

Unfortunately, it wasn't.

CHAPTER 23
I SNATCH DEFEAT FROM
THE JAWS OF VICTORY

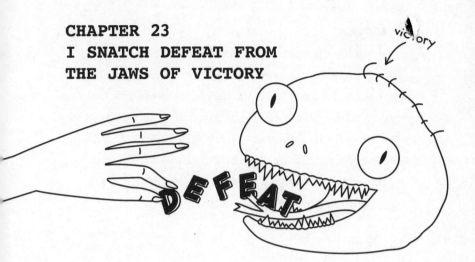

CLAUDIA

After Athena stormed out of the cafeteria, my Blurt nightmare SHOULD have been over.

But then Carmen got something in her eye.

CARMEN

I think it was just an eyelash. So it wouldn't have been a big deal. Except I just started wearing contact lenses. And when I rubbed my eye, the contact went somewhere weird. Like up in my eyelid or something.

CLAUDIA

Carmen started freaking out. So Parvati and Sophie and I went with her to the girls' bathroom to help get whatever it was out of her eye. We were all standing at the sink, and Carmen was holding up her eyelid, and Sophie was trying to look under it, and Carmen was going, "Do you see it? WHAT'S IN THERE?"

And then Parvati made a joke.

PARVATI

I said, "Maybe it's a thumb drive!" Which, hello? That was funny.

CLAUDIA

No, it wasn't. There was absolutely NOTHING funny about the Marcel situation.

But I should've just ignored Parvati instead of getting mad and telling her to be quiet. Because when I did, Carmen and Sophie realized Parvati and I were keeping some kind of major secret and insisted we absolutely had to tell them what we were talking about.

PARVATI

Can I just say, I would NOT have told them if you hadn't said it was okay?

CLAUDIA

I did NOT say it was okay! I just didn't say it WASN'T okay.

Either way, Parvati wound up telling Carmen and Sophie all about what happened at BlurtUp. Including the fact that the Lovefighters were trying to hunt me down.

And Parvati can be very loud.

And because we were in an eyeball-related hurry when we went into the bathroom, none of us had bothered to check under the stalls to see if anybody was inside one of them.

Like, say, a Fembot.

ALWAYS CHECK FOR LEGS BEFORE DISCUSSING
SENSITIVE INFORMATION IN GIRLS' BATHROOM

SOPHIE

So we hear a toilet flush, and all of a sudden Meredith Timms is standing there with this huge grin on her face, going, "OHMYGOSH I CANNOT BELIEVE THIS!"

CLAUDIA

Up until fifth grade, Meredith Timms was my best friend. But then she turned into a Fembot and completely blew me off, and it was totally devastating.

But that's a whole other story. I'm only mentioning it here because of what I said to Meredith in the bathroom.

CARMEN

You said something like, "Meredith, this is a VERY sensitive situation that could really hurt me, and if you ever cared AT ALL about our friendship, you would keep this between us and not tell anybody."

PARVATI

Meredith was all, "Mmmmmm-kay BYEEEEE!" Then she ran out of the bathroom. And BTW, she didn't wash her hands before she ran out. Which is TOTALLY GROSS!

CLAUDIA

When Meredith ran out of the bathroom, I actually thought for a minute she might keep my secret.

SOPHIE

I don't know why you thought that. Meredith's totally gone over to the Dark Side.

CLAUDIA

This is unfortunately true. By the time I got to the hallway where my locker is, Athena and the Fembots were waiting with big, evil grins on their faces.

And Athena said, "Here's the deal, loser: you have till 4:00pm TODAY to post a Blurt of you calling yourself the most basic idiot who ever lived...or I'll go on Marcel Mourlot's Blurt page and tell all the Lovefighters who you are and where you live."

Then they all cackled like hyenas and went to class.

FEMBOT CACKLING
LIKE A HYENA
(actual hyena)

CARMEN

I can NOT believe how vile they are.

PARVATI

I think they need a new nickname. "Fembots" isn't NEARLY evil enough.

CLAUDIA

That whole morning in class, it was pretty much impossible to focus on anything except my impending doom. I had to decide whether to completely humiliate myself or let an angry mob of strangers destroy me.

Except when I really thought about it, humiliating myself wasn't a choice at all. Even if I posted the Blurt, Athena would still be able to bust me with the Lovefighters any time she wanted. Knowing Athena, I figured she'd keep on blackmailing me with that forever. And there was no way I could let her have that kind of power.

So I was going to have to take my chances with the Lovefighters. Since Athena had given me until 4:00pm to post the Blurt, I had some time to try to minimize the damage. It was like having a weather

forecast that a hurricane was coming. You
can't stop the hurricane, but at least you
can tape up your windows and go hide in
the basement.

Which in this case meant deleting
all my social media accounts and trying
to get rid of every single photo of myself
that ever existed online. That way, nobody
could find one and Photoshop my head onto
dog poop. (or worse)

So when I got to the cafeteria for
lunch, I asked my friends to go through
their ClickChat pages and delete any photos
they'd posted that had me in them.

CARMEN

I never realized how many of my
photos you were in until you asked me to
delete them all. It was going to be a TON
of work.

PARVATI

It was going to be SO much work! So I
was like, "Why can't you just ask Marcel to
tell the Lovefighters to back off? They'll
do anything he says!"

CLAUDIA

As soon as Parvati said that, I realized it was a brilliant idea.

PARVATI

It wasn't brilliant. I was just being lazy. 'Cause I didn't want to deal with going through all my ClickChat photos.

CLAUDIA

It wasn't necessarily easy to get in touch with Marcel. The only email on his Blurt page was for "business," which didn't seem right. And I could Direct Message him, but with thirty million followers, he probably got a TON of DMs.

I decided to do both. And since there were only fifteen minutes left in lunch, I had to move fast.

I got out my phone and DM'ed Marcel, then copied the DM and sent it to his business email.

Dear Marcel,

I am the person who hurt your eye at BlurtUp on Saturday.

I am so so very very sorry for this!!!! I wanted to give you a thumb drive with some of my music on it, but I couldn't get close enough, so I threw it at the stage. I did NOT mean to hit you! Especially in the eye. I just wanted you to hear my music.

I am SO SORRY I scratched your cornea! If you tell me how much the doctor bill was, I will figure out how to pay you back for it.

Also, you may have noticed that a lot of Lovefighters in the comments are trying to figure out who I am so they can destroy me.

I know I kind of deserve it, but I'd really appreciate it if you could ask them to go easy on me. My brother just got attacked last week by a bunch of Bewbees, and it was very scary for my whole family.

I am going to delete my Blurt account in a few hours, so I hope you see this before then!!!

Sorry again! I hope your eye feels better!!!

Sincerely,

Claudia Tapper (@claudaroo)

CARMEN

That was an excellent apology.

CLAUDIA

Thanks. I actually felt better after I wrote it. But not THAT much better. Because mostly, all I could think about was the angry mob of Lovefighters. I kept checking my Blurt account between classes that afternoon, but I didn't hear anything back from Marcel.

And as the afternoon went on, I started to think I was insane to believe that Marcel would actually read my DM and save me from his angry Lovemob.

So when Athena walked by my locker after school and said, "Are you going to post the Blurt? Or am I going to send the Lovefighters after your sorry butt?" I told her to wait until 4:00, then check my Blurt page.

Which wasn't going to exist at 4:00, because I was going to delete it forever as soon as I got home.

But by the time I got there, everything had changed again.

CHAPTER 24
THE FRENCH GUY
GETS INVOLVED

CLAUDIA

    Parvati's text—which I got while I was walking down West End Avenue to my apartment—was my first hint that Marcel had gotten my DM.

PARVATI AND CLAUDIA (text messages)

EEEEEEEEEEEE!!!!!!!!!!

YOU'RE FAMOUS!!!!!

OMG DONT DELETE YR BLURT PAGE!!!!!!

CLAUDIA

I opened up Blurt, and the first thing I noticed was that I'd just gotten almost 1,000 new followers.

The second thing I noticed was that one of my weeks-old "Windmill" Blurts suddenly had 75,000 Blips.

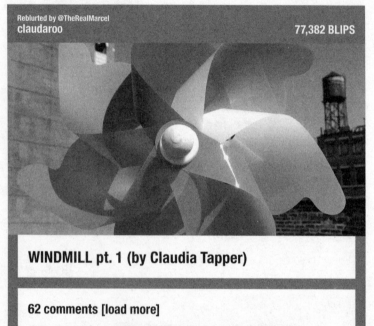

Reblurted by @TheRealMarcel
claudaroo

77,382 BLIPS

WINDMILL pt. 1 (by Claudia Tapper)

62 comments [load more]

@TheRealMarcel **HEY LOVEFIGHTERS CHECK OUT @claudaroo VIDEO AMAZING CLAUDIA TAPPER WILL BE A STAR AND CHANGE THE WORLD FOR SURE CHECK IT OUT!!!**

He also replied to my DM.

@THEREALMARCEL TO @CLAUDAROO (Blurt Direct Message)

THANK U FOR WRITING UR HONESTY IS SO BEAUTIFUL I CAN TELL U HAVE A GREAT SOUL

AND UR SONG WINDMILL IS AMAZING!! I LOVE IT I JUST RBD ONE OF UR BLURTS

MY EYE WILL BE FINE DONT WORRY

ALSO DONT WORRY ABOUT LOVEFIGHTERS THEY ARE ALL BEAUTIFUL AND ONLY WANT HAPPINESS FOR EVERYONE

PARVATI

OMG I CAN'T BELIEVE MARCEL DM'ED YOU!!!! You should totally print the screenshot and frame it. IN GOLD!!!!

CLAUDIA

The rest of my day—actually, my whole week—was amazingly great. Instead of spending it trying to delete all traces of myself from the Internet before the Lovefighters could destroy me, I got to spend it watching my "Windmill" Blurt hit 2,000,000 Blips and my followers increase to almost 9,000 people.

I also got to watch Athena make a complete fool of herself in Marcel's comment section.

BLURT COMMENT SECTION

426 comments [load more]

@FlorisDiz this song is great tbh click the link

@NJLoveFighter COOL VID @claudaroo LOVE UR SINGING

Athena

@goddessgurrl LOVEFIGHTERS!!!! @claudaroo IS THE PERSON WHO HIT MARCEL IN THE EYE AT BLURTUP!!!

@luvfitr100 jealous much?

@goddessgurrl ITS TRUE I GO TO SCHOOL WITH HER THAT BLACK/WHITE SKIRT IN THE PIC @FlorisDiz POSTED IS DEF HERS AND TOTALLY BASIC

@NJLoveFighter @goddessgurrl theres no way thats true Marcel just RBd her

@FlorisDiz thats ridic I don't even no u @goddessgurrl

@goddessgurrl LOVEFIGHTERS WHATS UR PROBLEM @claudaroo IS CLAUDIA TAPPER OF NYC AND SHE HURT MARCEL U NEED TO DESTROY HER!!!!!

@goddessgurrl SHE GOES TO CULVERT PREP AND HER HOME ADDRESS IS 437 WEST END AVENUE NYC

@FormrBlbr what is ur problem @goddessgurrl???? U r sick

@NJLoveFighter yah get off this thread @goddessgurrl u a creepy hater

@MarcelLoveFighter @goddessgurrl u must be jelly cuz @claudaroo is great

@FormrBlbr go back under ur bridge u troll @goddessgurrl

@goddessgurrl YOU ARE ALL IDIOTS

EPILOGUE

CLAUDIA

In case you were wondering if Marcel's RB'ing me meant that "Windmill" went viral, and millions of people listened to it, and it became a huge hit and launched my career as a famous singer-songwriter...that did not exactly happen.

The Blurt he RB'ed wound up getting millions of Blips, but most of the people who watched it never clicked over to listen to the whole song on MeVid. As of today, about 75,000 people have watched my "Windmill" video.

YAY!!! **76,167 Views**

Which is awesome! I am very, very happy about this. And I am totally grateful to Marcel Mourlot, not just for saving me from certain doom, but for getting the word out about my music. Even though it turns out

THINGS MARCEL
HAS RB'D IN
LAST 24 HOURS:
—baby licking
   pit bull
—man falling
   off couch
—3 singer-
   songwriters
   (1 great, 2 ok)
—4 comedians
   (2 funny)
—5 energy drink
   ads (pretty sure
   he got paid
   for these)
—woman burping
   national anthem

he RBs about twenty other people and/or companies every day.

The truth is, 75,000 views on MeVid might sound like a lot...but there are SO MANY people on the Internet that it's not all that amazing. For example, my guitar teacher, Randy, has been putting his own songs on MeVid for years. And his most popular one got TEN TIMES as many views as "Windmill"... and it STILL wasn't a hit.

RANDY

Kid, I am ALL kinds of proud of you. 75,000 views your first time out is an amazing start! But you gotta remember, I racked up 900,000 with "Rusty Heart." And I'm still teaching 12-year-olds how to play guitar. So you gotta keep it in perspective.

Now go write some more songs that knock everybody's socks off.

CLAUDIA

I will, Randy. Thanks for believing in me.

While I'm thanking people, I'd
also like to give a shout out to my
brother for letting me interview him
about what was basically the worst
experience of his life.

(+ post
embarrassing
dog pics)

REESE

It was pretty bad for a while there.
But eventually, the Bewbees got bored and
started hassling somebody else. So it's
fine now. Except I still can't post any pics
of myself on ClickChat, or somebody will
turn my face into a dog poop meme in about
thirty seconds.

Also, Xander wouldn't talk to me for a
couple days after Mom called Mrs. Billington
and told her what happened.

XANDER

Snitchin' on me wuz WEAK, yo! Mom-a-
saurus done come down hard! She took my
phone away three whole days!

CLAUDIA

Three days of no phone? After all the
trouble you got Reese into? Xander, that is
REALLY not harsh. At all.

REESE

Seriously, dude. That's like the opposite of harsh.

XANDER

It was gonna be a month. But Mom-a-saurus can't stay mad at her X-Boy. 'Specially after I was all, "Yo, I learned a valuable lesson from this!"

CLAUDIA

Really? This book's all about valuable lessons. What was yours?

XANDER

NO SNITCHIN'!!!!

CLAUDIA

(sarcasm)

Thanks, Xander. That's incredibly helpful.

REESE

You know what's really scary about the Internet? I spend, like, half my life on it. But I have NO CLUE how it even works.

And I kinda feel like Mom and Dad have even less of a clue.

DAD AND MOM (text messages)

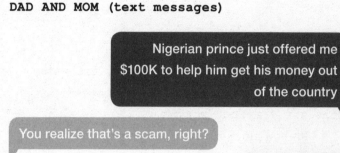

> Nigerian prince just offered me $100K to help him get his money out of the country

> You realize that's a scam, right?

> Of course I do

> I'm not completely stupid

> Also the link in the email he sent was broken

> OMG PLEASE TELL ME YOU DIDN'T CLICK THE LINK

Dad clicked link, got virus, had to buy new laptop + change his credit card numbers ☹ ☹ ☹

CLAUDIA

That's a very good point. And definitely scary. I don't really know how the Internet works, either.

REESE

Maybe we should make a pact to, like, not go online AT ALL until we know how it works.

CLAUDIA

That's a great idea. Except...if we're not on the Internet, we can't google "How does the Internet work?"

So how do we figure out the Internet without the Internet?

REESE

Oh, man...This is going to be hard.

IF YOU UNDERSTAND HOW THE INTERNET WORKS,
PLEASE WRITE TO US AT:

CLAUDIA (AND/OR REESE) TAPPER
c/o LITTLE, BROWN BOOKS FOR YOUNG READERS
1290 SIXTH AVENUE
NEW YORK, NY 10104
U.S.A.

THANKS FOR READING!!!

SPECIAL THANKS

Eliav Malone, Aden Malone, Liz Casal, John Hughes, Allegra Wertheim, Andy White, Nadia Vynnytsky, Brittney Morello, Trevor Williams, Daniella Sarnoff, John Malone, Jim Conant, Mike Thruman, Ali Benjamin, Tal Rodkey, Ronin Rodkey, Rahm Rodkey, Dafna Sarnoff, Andrea Spooner, Russ Busse, and Josh Getzler.

ABOUT THE AUTHOR

Geoff Rodkey is the author of the *New York Times* bestseller *The Tapper Twins Go to War (With Each Other)*, *The Tapper Twins Tear Up New York*, and *The Tapper Twins Run for President*, as well as the acclaimed adventure-comedy trilogy The Chronicles of Egg. He wrote the screenplays for the hit films *Daddy Day Care*, *RV*, and the Disney Channel's *Good Luck Charlie, It's Christmas!*, and has also written for the educational video game *Where in the World Is Carmen Sandiego?*, the non-educational MTV series *Beavis and Butt-Head*, Comedy Central's *Politically Incorrect*, and at least two magazines that no longer exist.

Geoff currently lives in New York City with his wife and three sons, none of whom bear any resemblance whatsoever to the characters in The Tapper Twins.

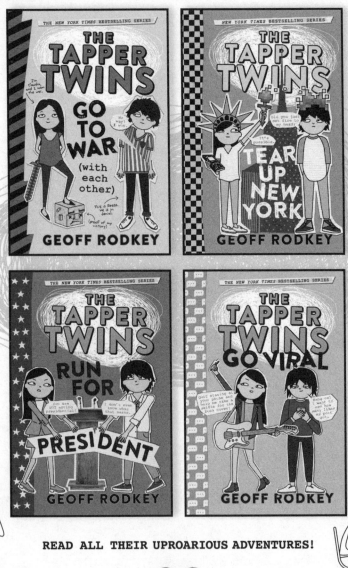